力得文化
Leader Culture

Lead your way. Be your own leader!

力得文化
Leader Culture

Lead your way. Be your own leader!

The Whole Package

力得文化
Leader Culture

導遊、領隊

Theodore◎著

FUN 英語

道地口語讓你
沉浸在旅遊樂趣裡

23 主題單元+附錄

嚴選地點： 驚奇美西、熱力關島、浪漫夏威夷、德國美景、日本嚴選、戀戀韓風、
台灣趣旅、福建遺產、絕色長灘島、奢華峇里、頂級馬新水上樂園等等

▷【情境對話】詼諧幽默、出人意表
▷【單詞與句型】配以道地的影集引述句 與眾不同、生動有趣
▷【達人提點】為導遊實際體驗 包羅萬象、應有盡有
▷【附錄】含行前攜帶物品一覽表 精采絕倫、無所不包
▷【號外】作者臉書附各式景點照片 詳情請見書中內文

MP3

由國際領隊執筆，
文中到訪之地，也是許多人旅遊必去之處，
國家從美、德、日、韓到台灣、新加坡和印尼無所不包，
讀者在閱讀對話的同時彷彿自己也開啟了一趟知性之旅。

作者序
Introduction

首先要感謝觀光領隊協會副理事長辛文義老師的引薦及雄獅導領部經理林正雄先生的提攜，沒有你們就沒有這本書。

如果不是從小開始學的語言，實在不太容易用該語言當母語思考，本書把日常生活中常見的思維，用簡單生動的道地美語勾勒出來，而且先研究不傷身體，希望大家不要學的太累，再講究效果，藉例句得到更多樣的表達能力。是不是有些英文書我們買回家後，常了翻幾頁就擱在那裏，三不五時還要時時勤拂拭，但是美劇跟電影卻多能看完？所以此書一開始的設計就以故事性的方式，由人與人間的互動為出發點，希望讀者會看到最後一章。書中精彩實用的內容，就像夏夜裡數不盡的繁星，又像陽春麵裡挑不完的蔥，隨便翻一頁吧！

To 林檎さん,
You made me a better person.

Theodore

編者序
WORDS FROM EDITOR

全書分為四大部分，內容覆蓋中、美、德、日、韓、臺灣、新加坡和印尼等等。讀者在閱讀對話的同時彷彿暢遊了一趟世界之旅。

有限的篇幅裡，編者在地點的取捨上可謂是煞費心思，希望能給讀者體現最具代表性的內容。文中到訪之處，多是各大旅行社的熱門景點，大家若曾出國旅遊或上線帶團的話，相信必不陌生。

【情境對話】裡作者鮮明的描繪了領隊跟旅客間人性化、多樣化相處的方式。時而如保姆般語重心長、耳提面命，時而如班上活寶般搞笑無厘頭。書中的對話內容跌宕起伏，各種角色躍然紙上如在眼前，也使得對話更具可看性。

【單詞與句型】中除了各種信手拈來的生活美語與中文，更有著如史詩般的詳解。同時，開外掛附上了從海量影集中精挑細選出來的例句，讓讀者在用不同方式對照比較加深印象的同時，也發現說英文原來可以像說中文這麼帶感！

【達人提點】包含了作者旅居國外的深度體驗，帶團走馬看花的各種提點。從美景、美食、美酒、風俗民情、中西文化、美制單位等包羅萬象，更有過來人的心情故事。

【附錄】為作者細心與體貼表露無遺的行李打包術，相信您會跟我一樣喜歡這道私房菜。

力得文化編輯群

CONTENTS ✈ 目次

AIRPORT

PART 1
歐美豪華之旅

1.1 發現美西‧驚奇美西 賭城夜遊、自費活動

情境對話

 MP3 001

麥可
再見了！快樂狗鬼城，現在車子左轉上交流道了。
Adios! Calico ghost town, now the bus turns left and takes on-ramp.

麥可
接下來，我們奔向紙醉金迷的賭城。
Next, we're heading to the extravagant Vegas.

麥可
隨著夜幕低垂，拉斯維加斯越夜越美麗。
As the evening progresses, the Vegas is more dramatic in the darkness.

麥可
視覺效果只能用不可思議來形容。
The visual effects are magical in every sense of the word.

麥可
還有精彩無比奧運級的表演。
And the most amazing Olympic-Class performance.

麥可
我們應該在兩個半小時之內就到了。
We should be there within two and half an hour.

麥可
大家可以看看窗外沿途的風景，或閉上眼睛休息一下。
You can look at the interstate out the window, or close your eyes and take a nap.

Rachel
麥可講笑話。
Michael tell us a joke.

麥可
嗯？好der，很久很久以前，有兩個…
Eh? All right, once upon a time, there were two…

Barney
要怎麼學點英文？！
How do we learn some English?!

麥可
是的，很久很久以前…
Okay, once upon a time…

Rachel
麥可用英文講笑話！
Michael tells a joke in English!

麥可
這個之前是…萬一司機笑壞了，忍不住舉雙手歡呼，這主意不太妙。
Well, What if the driver cracks up, raises his hands, and whoops! I don't think this is a good idea.

麥可
關於拉斯維加斯，有沒有聽過一句話叫…
About Vegas, Have you ever heard the saying…

麥可
過去的就讓它過去，曾經畢竟只是曾經。
What happens in Vegas stays in Vegas.

麥可
舞台只是古往今來芸芸眾生的縮影。
What happens in Vegas happens in more places than Vegas.

Rachel
活在當下！
Viva La Vida!

Barney
假掰文青！
Hipster scum!

麥可
好極了！好個活在當下。
Wally-kazam! Viva La Vida there it is.

 麥可
天增歲月人增壽，難得放鬆來看秀。
Time flies wrinkles in the eye, lay back, and live in style.

 麥可
走過路過別錯過，賺錢就是要享受！
We're not here but passing by, kiss your money and say goodbye!

 Rachel
姐要是看過茱比莉秀這輩子也值了！（嗚嗚～）
I wouldn't miss Jubilee for the world! *sob sob*

 Rachel
不然我可白來一趟拉斯維加斯了。
Otherwise what happens in Vegas won't happen to me.

 Barney
我要看王子秀跟水秀。
I wanna see the KA Show and the O Show.

 麥可
請把這張活動報名表傳下去。
Please pass this activity sign-up sheet.

 麥可
下車前要確定參加人數。
We have to make sure of the final head count before getting off the bus.

 麥可
在你的右手邊是這裡的地標可樂世界。
On your right is the landmark Coca-Cola World.

 麥可
旅館離這裡5分鐘。兩天都住同一家，不用收行李。
The hotel is 5 minutes away. We are staying in the same one for two days. We don't have to pack.

 Barney
我今晚要盛裝出席盡情搖擺！
I'll suit up and turn my swag on tonight!

Rachel

搖咧～搖咧～有人自告奮勇帶動氣氛啦～
YEARHHH~ YEARHHH~ Someone gets the point and is going wild~

✓ 再見了 "adios"

西班牙語的再見，Adiós [ˌɑ•dɪˈos]，其他常見的還有在其他chapter裡會提的義大利語ciao，剛開始不熟忘記的時候可以這麼聯想，收音機的複數Radios去掉前面那個R就是adios了 ^^

拜拜，萌妹紙！（ 近音字 muchacho[muˈtʃɑ•tʃo] 正太 ）

Adios, muchacha!

—— 《*How I Met Your Mother 05x15 Rabbit Or Duck*》

✓ 上交流道，入口匝道 "takes on-ramp"

→ 用on-off不用in-out。

有人錯過了交流道！

Somebody missed the off-ramp!

—— 《*Friends 03x07 The Race Car Bed*》

你忘了下交流道。

You missed the exit.

—— 《*Friends 03x06 The Flashback*》

✅ 奢侈的，浪費的 "extravagant"

強調的是「可惜了」

去拉斯維加斯是不是奢侈了點。

Going to Las Vegas seems a bit extravagant.

—— 《Everybody Loves Raymond 07x06 Robert Needs Money》

有點奢侈但我談到了很好的價錢。

It was extravagant, but I got a good deal.

—— 《Friends 05x21 The One With The Ball》

✅ 貴三三 "luxurious [lʌgˈʒʊ•rɪəs]"

強調的是那個奢侈奢華的金碧輝煌的畫面感。

但有時候，一點奢侈是必要的。

But sometimes a little luxury is necessary.

—— 《Everybody Loves Raymond 01x08 In-Laws》

我沒有朋友這種奢侈品。

I don't have the luxury of friends.

—— 《Batman Begins 2005》

✅ 過去的，曾經 "What happens in Vegas."

這句話有很多意思，也有很多變化，先説有安慰人心的意思，比如在賭城輸多了，就把這不舒服的回憶留在拉斯維加斯，離開了就別再去想了。"Suck it up and move on, you don't need to carry the memories with you." 事情過了就過了，不要有罣礙，這個這個…心如澄澈秋水，泛若不繫之舟的感覺有莫有（繫跟夕讀同音），同樣的句型換了那個Vegas，提醒對方這件事這裡説了這裡算，別張揚的意思。

我這麼說吧，華盛頓的事，就讓它留在華盛頓，嗯？
Can I just say, what happens in Washington, stays in Washington, yeah?

—— 《*In The Loop 2009*》

我有一個原則，加長型禮車內的事不外傳。
I've got a code. What happens in the limo, stays in the limo.

—— 《*Modern Family 02x15*》

你在這裡說的話會被保密，所以這裡才叫做安全地帶。
What happens in Safe Place stays in Safe Place. That's why it's called Safe Place.

—— 《*Orange Is The New Black 02x11 Take A Break From Your Values Proper*》

✔地標 "landmark"

問路除了問路名，通常我們也會問指標性建築物，一個landmark搞定了。 ‹cf.› 別說成obvious building。

那所豪宅是一處具有歷史化價值的地標建築。
That mansion is a historical and cultural landmark...

—— 《*Miss March*》

✔奧運級的 "Olympic-Class"

關於跟什麼同等級的幾個說法。除了什麼-Class，也有用什麼-strength，什麼-grade，什麼-quality。

我發簡訊跟她說你需要浣腸劑，這是超重口的手帕交私房話吧。

I texted her and said you needed an enema. Okay, now, this is some industrial-strength girl talk.

—— 《2 Broke Girls 02x09》

當然了，我和一些專業級的雞尾酒專家一起去派對。

I do! I went to a party with a professional-grade margarita machine.

—— 《Cougar Town 1x05》

跳樓大拍賣，這價值像白粉那麼貴的畫，只賣跟白菜一樣的價錢。

Gallery-quality paintings at sidewalk prices.

—— 《Bobs Burgers 01x08》

✅ 講笑話 "tell a joke, break a jest"

到哪裡玩都免不了拉車，歐洲十天玩三國的，坐車時間更短不了，有時候沿路講解，有時候就讓客人多睡一下。專業導覽當然是美事一椿，但走火入魔就有點那個啥了，可別把睡覺的客人搖醒說：「喂車上不准睡！專心聽我導覽！」^^

✅ 笑點／梗／笑柄 "punch line"

好吧，笑點在哪裡？

All right, what's the punch line?

—— 《Everybody Loves Raymond 08x21 The Model》

媽，這笑話我不說了，因為你破梗了！

Ma, I'm not telling the joke, because you blew the punch line!

—— 《Everybody Loves Raymond 05x20 Net Worth》

不許你再破別人笑話的梗了。

You don't say the punch lines to other people's jokes anymore.

—— 《Bobs Burgers 01x09》

她說的其實是面子。同時，她在網上成了笑柄了。

Honor, actually, is what she said. Meanwhile, she's a punch line on the Internet.

—— 《The Newsroom 01x06》

劇透 "spoiler / ruin the ending"

但是最糟最糟的部分在結局。他們在婚禮上… 哇哦！劇透！

But the worst, the worst was the ending. So they're at the wedding... Whoa-oh! Spoilers!

—— 《How I Met Your Mother 05X23 The Wedding Bride》

很多盡在不言中。就像有次，一個女孩跟我說。警告！劇透慎入喔。

There's a lot unsaid. Like one time, a girl said to me. Warning! Spoiler alert.

—— 《New Girl 01x11》

別了，不許劇透。我還沒看第三季呢。

Hold up. No spoilers. I haven't started season three yet.

—— 《2 Broke Girls 02x16》

你確定要讓我劇透嗎？

Are you sure you want me to ruin the ending?

—— 《Boardwalk Empire 1x09 Belle Femme》

我不想劇透。

I don't want to give away the ending.

—— 《Be Wtih You 01x06》

✔ 盡情搖擺 "swag"

每個人今晚都把自己最有魅力的一面釋放出來！swag，個人魅力，範兒，就愛他那調調兒，漂丿，帥勁。swag用的很浮濫，就跟rocket science，so true一樣，也有人特別看不慣，就挖苦這字是Secretly We Are Gays的縮寫。

大家來跳舞！來跟我跳舞！我要跳出我的風格！

Everyone dance! Dance with me! Turn my swag on!

—— 《Skins 05x07 Grace》

嗯，如果你要是想說有點太招搖，那你就對了！

Yeah, if you mean a little much swagger, you got that right!

—— 《Orange Is The New Black 02x07 Comic Sans》

✔ 報名表 "sign-up sheet"

報名表單／參加表。

近音字 簽到單，打卡"Sign-in sheet"。

來吧，瘦身的最好方法就是加入舞蹈校隊。報名表剛出來。

Come on, best way to tighten up a tummy is varsity dance team. The sign-up sheet just went up.

—— 《Kick-Ass 2 2013》

我們在登記簿上看到了你的名字，我們想知道你記不記得，在你前面一個用電腦的人是誰。

We got your name from the sign-in sheet, and we were wondering if you can remember, who was using that computer right before you.

—— 《*Hawaii Five O 02x13*》

✅ 自告奮勇 "takes the point"

take point，walk point，尖兵，打前哨，身先士卒，一馬當先。

重複，你們可以出發了 好的，我們打前鋒！

Repeat, you have a go! Okay! We'll take point!

—— 《*Stargate 01x05 The Broca Divide*》

提雅克，帶路，皮爾斯，你斷後。羅斯曼，你跟著我。

Teal'c, take point. Pierce, you got our six. Rothman, you're with me.

—— 《*Stargate 04x08 The First Ones*》

我來打頭陣。威爾斯，博斯沃你們做後衛。間距5米散開。

I'll take point. Wells, Bosworth, you're rear guard. Five-meter spread.

—— 《*Stargate 07X17 Heroes-Part 1*》

👍 達人提點

✅ 要怎麼學點英文 "How to learn some English"

傳統方式可以參考不用拘泥

線上字典只能查個概念，有時候它的解釋跟例句都看得很累，甚者有的字典上那些N年前的例句跟N平方年前的解釋與現今的語言差了NN次方公里。

善用搜尋飛花落葉可以為劍

英英字典會比較好，是的，有時候也用英英，英英字典好。問題是如果每個人都是一直是用英英字典學的話，那誰還用學了，幾個蝙蝠俠受的鳥只看英英啊？而且有時這個英文的意思是懂了，但是用中文卻不知怎麼表達這也是個問題，人生苦短說點簡單實際的好不。推薦搜尋圖片，一眼瞄了個過去幾十張圖，用右腦接受圖像概念，那效果反而勝過千言萬語 "It's worth a billion words."

搜影片也是一個很好的方式，去知名影片網站搜下本書中提到的關鍵字 "Obama Michelle Fist Bump"，看一下10秒的片子，你就知道fist bump是什麼意思什麼感覺了，不但印象更深刻，影片還有一個好處就是，有些發音字典上查不到的，例如這逆天的麵疙瘩好不容易翻成Chinese Gnocchi [no•kɪ]，然後怎麼唸呢？就算用線上翻譯找到義大利語發音，美國人也不一定聽的懂什麼意思，直接去影片網站看一下美國人怎麼唸的，就照他們這樣念囉。對了有個叫VoiceTube的網站不錯，有美劇影音例句喔。 :D

1.2 發現美西・驚奇美西 大峽谷天空步道、印地安風味餐

💬 情境對話

 MP3 002

麥可：好，現在我們在往大峽谷的路上。
All right, now we're traveling to the Grand Canyon.

我們過了臭屁卡拿路，也就是內華達593號州公路。
We went through Tropicana Avenue, which is the Nevada State Route 593.

走93號國道。
Take Highway 93.

對了，秀看的怎麼樣？
BTW, how was the show?

好的不可思議！
Marvelous!

好看吼。是啊，到賭城錯過看秀太可惜了。
Nice show huh. You bet, you wouldn't miss that for the world.

那到大峽谷你就要體驗一下，在天空步道上，以720度的視野看大峽谷的感覺。
In the Grand Canyon, you must experience the 720 degree view of the Canyon from Skywalk.

昨天有人買可樂護唇膏嗎？
Anyone buy a Coke Biggy yesterday?

麥可

有！
Here!

Rachel

什麼護唇膏？
What's a Coke Biggy?

Carolyn

是可口可樂口味的一種護唇膏。
Some Coca Cola lip care.

Rachel

我買了很多，你要幾個？
I bought a lot, how many do you want?

Rachel

我跟你買兩個好了，謝謝。
I'd like to buy two of them from you, thanks.

Carolyn

我們等下在休息站換車後，前往我樂派印第安保留區。
Later after changing vehicles at the rest stop, and we will be heading to Hualapai Indian Reservation.

麥可

然後往北走到皮爾斯港口路，也就是25號縣道的盡頭。
Then we'll going northeast on Pierce Ferry Road, that is County Highway 25.

麥可

中午享用風味餐，大家很快就可以跟原住民見面了。
After having ethnic food for lunch, we'll meet up with some native people.

麥可

請問他們是說英語嗎？
May I ask if they speak English?

Carolyn

是的，他們會說英語。恩…你有什麼事情要問這些印第安人嗎？
Yes, they speak English. Well...Do you have any question to ask those American Indians?

麥可

Carolyn
沒有。
Nope.

麥可
其實近來印第安人講的是中文…
Natives actually speak Chinese these days…

Carolyn
蝦毀！？
Say what!?

麥可
咳咳。各位，注意聽好。
Ahem. Folks, listen up.

麥可
當到達我樂派印第安保留區以後，來個約法三章喔，就是，有些事不可以做。
When we reach Hualapai Indian Reservation, there are some certain rules, you know, dos and don'ts.

麥可
請一定要遵守規定。
You have to observe the rules, please.

麥可
最近因為華人遊客眾多，必須保護我樂派的傳統文化。
Recently a lot of Chinese-speaking tour groups have visited, so Hualapai culture and traditions must be carefully preserved.

麥可
所以當地政府立了一個嚴禁觀光客教印第安人說中文的政策，這樣大家都明白了嗎？
So the Nevada Government has a very strict No-Teaching-Indians-Mandarin policy, do you understand?

Rachel
真的假的？！
Really?!

Carolyn
起笑！亂講，這一定是麥可亂講的。
That's crazy talk! Baloney, don't listen to Michael.

☆ 單詞與句型

✔593號州公路 "State Route 593"

593號州內公路。縮寫為SR 593。**比較** 州際公路是Interstate。公路用 Route。在593號公路上，用on。**例如** On Route 593。

你知道我們在幾號公路上嗎？

Do you know what route we're on?

我們在27號公路一個休息站。

We are at a rest stop on Route 27.

—— 《*Friends 03x17 Without The Ski Trip*》

✔93號國道 "US Highway 93"

其他跟公路交通相關的。

➡ **"Turnpike" 收費公路**
一個要付費的快速道路 "A toll expressway"。你要pay a toll才能drive on a turnpike。

➡ 過路費 **"Toll fee"**

➡ 回數票 **"Toll tickets"**
比較 買黃牛票"Buy resale tickets"。黃牛 "Scalper"。

➡ 收費站 **"Toll station / toll gate"**

➡ 收費亭 **"Toll booth / tollbooth"**
講到booth第一個會想到電話亭 "A phone booth"，機場裡那種快速照相的小房間叫 "Photo booth"。舞廳裡的DJ台 "DJ booth"。餐廳或夜店裡，一格一格的開放式半隔間座位區，半包雅座。介系詞用in，在

第二桌 "In booth two"。

收票員，好乏味的工作。

Tollbooth operator. That's a lonely line of work.

—— 《Fringe 01x19》

抓超速的 "a speed trap"

那裡有一個測速點 "There's a speed trap there." 超速 "Violate the speed limit"，超速駕駛人 "Speeder"。講到speeder順便提一下迪士尼卡通裡的大笨狼與嗶嗶鳥 "Wile E. Coyote and Road Runner"。有些經典的美國影片或卡通，就算已經很久很舊了，也仍然活在人心裡，成為美國庶民文化的一部分。然後這隻大笨狼每次抓嗶嗶鳥都失敗。失敗的方式各種不同，最常見的橋段就是追著追著一把抓空以後，掉到像我們今天參觀的大峽谷 "The Grand Canyon" 裡了。

三角錐，障礙錐 "traffic cone / safety cones"

玩賽車遊戲時常撞飛的那個東西，美語中也常用來形容胸前偉大。

你胸前那兩個看起來像巨無霸橘色障礙錐的，是在告訴我此處不准停車嗎？

Those look like two giant orange traffic cones. Are you trying to tell me not to park there?

—— 《2 Broke Girls 1x17 And The Kosher Cupcakes》

那是很尖銳的胸罩。 我知道，就像見鬼的交通三角錐。

That is a sharp, pointy bra. I know. They're like frickin' traffic cones.

—— 《Cougar Town 1x05》

✅ 交通管制 "traffic control"

常在飛機上聽到的，各位女士先生們：現在我們正在等待塔台允許起飛的命令。請不要離開座位並繫好安全帶，謝謝您的合作。"Ladies and gentlemen: we are now waiting for departure clearance from air traffic control tower. Please remain in your seats and fasten your seat belt, thanks for your cooperation." (航管：air traffic control；航管員：an air-traffic controller；塔台：the air-traffic control tower；機場地面台交通管制：airport ground traffic control)

我們提前十分鐘到達，但地勤沒有可用的登機口給我們。
We arrived 10 minutes early and ground traffic control doesn't have a gate for us.

—— 《The Newsroom 01x07》

✅ 路障，拒馬 "spiked barrier"

還有一種在停車場出入口的地上常看到，有個一整排看起來會戳破輪胎的尖尖的 "Automated spiked barrier"，中文是叫自動路障機，怎麼聽起來有點智障…通常用來管制車輛單向管制進出 "One way traffic control"。

✅ 高壓電塔 "pylon ['paɪ•lɑn]"

✅ 加油 "stop for gas / stop to get some gas / find a pit stop to refuel"

→ 加油站 "a pit stop / a petrol ['pɛ•trəl] station / a gas station"
我們開走了，We drive off。我們離開加油站，We pull out of a gas

station。（ **比較** 靠邊停，Pull over）

加油站是不允許吸煙的。

You shouldn't be smoking at a petrol station.

—— 《Banshee 02x06》

加油機 "pump"

大咖仔認為他有輛好車，然後他就能把車堵在加油機前面。

Big shot thinks he's got a fancy freakin' car and he can block the pump.

—— 《Banshee 02x06》

我神遊虛空了，因為在3號加油機加油那個男的，看起來像我的前男友。

I spaced out because the man at pump 3 looked just like my ex-boyfriend.

—— 《Devise-Wals Cd1》

加油站服務員 "the gas station attendant"

你用事業線從加油站店員那裡騙跳跳糖吃。

You used your boobs to get free pop rocks from the gas station attendant.

—— 《Be Wtih You 01X10》

換車 "changing vehicles"

換車，換路走，安全第一。

Switching up the cars, switching up the routes, just to be safe.

—— 《Person Of Interest 01X14》

靠邊停。在這里停。

Pull over. Pull over here.

安迪，你幹什麼？我們得換車！快。

Andy, what are you doing? We gotta do the switch! Let's go.

—— 《*Orange Is The New Black 02x08 Appropriately Sized Pots*》

✅ 在休息站 "at the rest stop"

停車休息十五分鐘，各位。我們中午之前就會抵達匹茲堡了。

15-minute rest stop, folks. We'll be in Pittsburgh before noon.

—— 《*Banshee 01x06*》

那邊有休息站。

There's a rest stop right up there.

—— 《*Friends 03X17 Without The Ski Trip*》

✅ 護唇膏 "lip care"

Lip Smacker是美國一個護唇膏的牌子，已成為護唇膏的代名詞，有各種口味，可樂口味的系列叫 "Coke Biggy"，這個系列有個禮盒 "Gift set" 6個一組，包裝就是個可樂罐。護唇膏還有很多種，下面括號裡的解釋是為了加深印象，只是個大概：lip balm（有的做得像個雞蛋）；lip salve（鞋油，粉餅的形狀）；lip ointment（膏狀的像牙膏擠出來）。

✅ 我樂派 "Hualapai"

念作Wal-lah-pie，是美洲印第安人的一支部落。

27

原住民 "aboriginal people"

例如 indigenous people [ɪnˈdɪ•dʒɪ•nəs]，people作為人的時候複數也是 people，不加s。作為民族時，複數加s表達不同族原住民的總稱，比如 九族文化村的九族。

他們也希望避免進一步的打擾當地的原住民。

They also want to avoid further upsetting the indigenous people.

—— 《Stargate 02x13 Spirits》

約法三章，公約規矩 "some certain rules"

如果他們想住在我的房子裡，是有些規矩。

If they want to live in my house, there are certain rules.

—— 《Everybody Loves Raymond 09x08》

遵守規定 "observe the rules"

observe有觀察，也有遵守的意思。邊觀察邊跟著人家這樣做，中文叫？ 入鄉隨俗 "Observe the customs"。

我們在人家的地盤，我們要入鄉隨俗。

We're in their country, we have to observe their customs.

—— 《Family Guy 09x07 Road To The North Pole》

亂講 "baloney"

baloney，除了香腸的意思之外，也作 "Holy crap, horse crap, nonsense" 胡扯淡的意思，這字這樣記，香腸你個芭樂胡説什麼，好記吧！^^ 她剛 才根本不知道自己在講什麼 "She didn't know what she was talking about." 你根本不知道自己在講什麼 "You don't know what you're talking about." 表達亂講，比較正經也很常用的一個說法是 "That's not true." 或 "You just made that up."

什麼算命都是騙人的。
Fortune-telling's a scam [skæm].

—— 《2 Broke Girls 02x15》

那個根本是胡說八道。
Oh, that's just gibberish ['dʒɪ•bə•rɪʃ].

—— 《Cougar Town 1x14》

你連說謊都不會。
You're a poor liar.

—— 《Arrow 01x05》

政策 "policy"

我們嚴禁寵物 "We have a strict no-pet policy." 我們的東西假一賠命 "We have a very strict no-copycat policy." 其他還可以用prohibited跟forbidden。

關於打火機

大部分國家隨身是可以帶一個，防風型打火機不行，不能放行李裡。但是美國TSA規定一個都不行，所以凡是飛美國的都不能帶打火機。

飛機上嚴禁攜帶打火機。
Lighters are strictly forbidden [fɚ'bɪ•dn] on the aircraft.

—— 《Bones 04x10》

他們擁有一拖拉庫被禁止持有的武器。

They have a hoard of prohibited [prə'hɪ•bɪ•tɪd] weaponry.

—— 《Stargate 03x02 Seth》

👍 達人提點

✅ 行程的掌握

交通的狀況難以掌握也是要掌握，看夕陽變看星星這是小事。本來行程的安排是避開交通尖峰時段，但是，班機誤點？行李遲到？遇上罷工？司機迷路？孩子不見？終於把烙賽的孩子從廁所找回來後，正面遇上大塞車，結果就是⋯四點午餐五點晚餐，旅館沒到司機下班。

我們早點出發避開交通尖峰時段。

Let's get an early start, we'll beat the crowds.

—— 《Our Idiot Brother》

✅ 超時工作

當天的行程走下來，比如早上八點半車輪子轉起來到晚上八點半回旅館，一天從招呼客人吃早餐上行李到回酒店查完房，有些導遊跟司機上下班還要坐或開一個小時車回去，隨隨便便都14、15個小時，連續幾天下來真的不輕鬆。

✅ 疲勞駕駛

一個昏昏欲睡的司機 "A drowsy driver" 怎麼能負責全車人員的安全，很多國家都嚴格規定不得疲勞駕駛 "Don't drive tired"。美國法律規定遊覽巴士的司機，包括遊客下車購物的等待時間，連續工作時間 "Continuous service" 不得超過8小時。不過美國的行車紀錄是司機自己寫的，所以啊這個…

✅歐美有別

歐洲就沒這麼好忽悠了，警察隨時都能查司機改不了的電子式行車紀錄器"Tachograph"（ 比較 轉速表：tachometer [tæ'kɑ•mɪ•tɚ]，時速表：speedometer [spɪ'dɑ•mɪ•tɚ]）。德國闖紅燈 "Run a red light" 零點幾秒記點罰錢，只要超過一秒不囉嗦扣駕照。所以超時工作就算多給錢也很多人不幹，因為被抓到的話畫面太美咱不敢看。

1.3 年輕熱力 關島六天四夜海底漫步 和高空跳傘

💬 情境對話

MP3 003

こごめさん 我等不及明天去玩海底漫步了。
I can't wait for the Sea Walk Tour tomorrow.

麥可 你有溯溪鞋嗎？
Did you bring your dive Boots?

こごめさん 不能光著腳走嗎？
Can't I walk barefoot?

麥可 你可以在海灘上光著腳丫走。
You can walk barefoot on the beach.

麥可 但海底有小石頭跟珊瑚可能會割傷你的腳。
But on the bottom of the sea, there are tiny bits of rocks and corals that might cut your feet.

こごめさん 懂了，我要穿泳裝嗎？
Got it, should I wear bikini?

麥可 泳裝或T恤短褲都可以。
Bikinis or T-shirts with shorts, both are fine.

こごめさん 我不會游泳又很怕死，怎麼辦？
I can't swim and I am not ready to die, now what?

你在頭盔裡就像在陸地上一樣的呼吸，不會有溺水或窒息的感覺。
You can breathe while wearing a mask. The same as you would on the land. You won't drown or choke.

當你下水的時候，氣壓的快速改變可能會引起你耳鳴。
When you get in the water, the rapid changes in air pressure might cause your ears to block.

閉上嘴巴，憋氣數到五。
Close your mouth and hold your breath for a count of five.

接著從鼻子往外吐氣，並且吞口水就好了。
Then breathe out through your nose, and swallow your saliva [sə'laɪ•və].

在海底有欄杆，你可以當作支撐扶著走。
On the bottom of the sea, handrails are provided. You can hold on to the rail as a support while walking.

情侶一起手牽手在海底漫步聽起來好幸福。
It sounds so wonderful that lovers walk hand in hand underwater.

就算一個人抓欄杆，也可以小小幻想一下撕床單的幸福。
Even holding the rail alone, there is nothing wrong with fantasizing about someone.

那不一樣好吧。
That's not exactly the same.

我想一下…有一種香艷刺激的雙人高空跳傘，你要參加嗎？
Let me think about this for a moment… It's thrill-seeking, and you got company, tandem skydiving, you in?

33

未滿18歲的需有父母或監護人的書面同意。
麥可 Passengers under 18 require written consent of a parent [pə'rɛn•t] or guardian.

如果有個萬一的話，你不太有可能在國外打官司。因此，我建議你買個全面的保險。
麥可 It is extremely unlikely that you will be able to sue anyone if you are injured overseas. So I recommend that you purchase full insurance.

恩，好。
こごめさん Well, okay.

體重要在100公斤以內才能參加。
麥可 Maximum weight for skydiving is 235lbs.

你這句話什麼意思？
こごめさん What's that supposed to mean?

沒-沒什麼意思。
麥可 N-nothing.

只是一句話而已。我剛才是說…
麥可 It's just an expression. I was like…

不用解釋了。我參加。
こごめさん Save it. I'm in.

那簽完這張生死狀就去那邊付錢。
麥可 Then sign up this waiver and pay over there.

有八千，一萬，一萬二，到一萬四千英呎，你要哪種？
麥可 Eight thousand, ten thousand, twelve thousand, fourteen thousand, your choice?

其實我越來越緊張了，八千英呎的就好了。
Actually, I'm kind of getting freak out. I'll say eight thousand.

接下來工作人員會教一些簡單的基本動作，請專心聽一下。
Next the staff will give some introductory training. Listen up, please.

嗨各位，我們接到機長的通知，由於天氣因素的關係，恭喜所有的人都免費升級到一萬四千英呎。
Hi all, we just get the notice from the captain regarding the weather. Congrates all of you on a free upgrade to a 14000 feet.

ㄟ害！
D'oh

✓ 海底漫步 "Sea Walk Tour"

一種帶著氧氣供應面罩在海底漫步的活動。**例如** Helmet dive，Sea Walker。

✓ 溯溪鞋 "Dive Boots"

另一種溯溪鞋Boots Rafting比較厚重。因為我也很少真的溯溪，在水裡有抓地力，保護腳底，不會掉，輕便易乾，對我來說穿 "Dive boots" 就可以了。溯溪，"Canyoning ['kæn•jə•nɪŋ]"，也做 "River trekking" 或 "River climbing"。

✅ 光著腳ㄚ走，光著腳走 "walk barefoot"

中間不用加上with或by。

✅ 短褲 "shorts"

→ **shorts**大部分時候的意思是 "**Short pants**"，短褲。
- Running shorts / gym shorts，運動短褲。
- Bike shorts / bicycle shorts，自行車短褲／單車褲。
- Swim shorts，泳褲。
- Board shorts，海灘褲。

→ **shorts**也指男生的內褲。

怎麼回事，克里斯？你拉在內褲裡了？

What's the matter, Chris? Shit hit your shorts?

—— 《Kick-Ass 2 2013》

我想是時候了。脫下你的小褲褲。

Okay, I guess it's time. Drop your shorts.

—— 《How I Met Your Mother 02x13 Columns》

✅ 熱褲

hot pants，hot就是熱，這個好記。

黑色上衣，黑色熱褲。

Black top, black hot pants.

—— 《Hawaii Five O 01x05》

"Daisy Dukes" 也是熱褲，這是從一個美國電視連續劇《正義前鋒。the

Dukes Of Hazzard。1979～1985》來的，裡面的Daisy Mae Duke（Catherine Bach飾）總喜歡穿著熱褲，後人為了紀念她，就以這個角色的名字 "Daisy Duke" 作為熱褲的代名詞。可能當時民風純樸，如今看Catherine Bach在片中穿的那短褲也就一般般，但是這個字已成為性感熱褲的代名詞，就像後面會提到的 "Short shorts" 一樣。

看看這個，這人到底是賣卡片還是熱褲？
Look at this. This guy selling cards or Daisy Dukes?
—— 《Chicago Pd 01x04》

"Short shorts"，短短褲，這個才是時尚時尚最時尚的超級熱褲。有些字典翻譯short shorts成美國婦女穿在外面的冬季短褲，應該是要加上winter，比如 "Winter short shorts" 或 "Short shorts for winter"。如果是沒有winter就只有short shorts的話，感覺就是那種露出南半球的 "Cheek shorts"。

穿著熱褲和蕾絲胸罩在他的房子裡跑來跑去，內褲都露出來了。
Running around his house in short shorts, lace bra, underwear hanging out.
—— 《Shameless Us 01x12》

✅ 女用內褲

《美國》Panties；《澳洲》undies；《英國》knickers（**比較** 燈籠褲：Knickerbockers ['nɪ•kə•ba•kə]，第一個K不發音）。

Boyshorts是一種低腰四角的女生內褲。並不是男生內褲的意思。Hipsters是三角的boyshorts。Hipster這個字是不是很眼熟？對，就是跟 "Hipster scum" 凹梨子文青的那個hipster同一個字。

✅ 男生內褲

→ **Men's briefs** 男用緊身三角褲。

· Boxer briefs / tight boxers，男用緊身四角褲。
· Boxer shorts，男用寬鬆四角褲。

近音字 "Man's briefcase" 男生的公事包。

感覺有點迷茫？這樣記，"Boxer" 就想到四角；"Briefs" 就想到緊身；"Shorts" 就想到寬鬆。帶團 "Running a tour" 穿什麼內褲好？這個問題問得好。出團的話如果該團是單男，那就跟領隊同一房，穿這種 "Boxer shorts" 比較方便。這樣大家都會買內褲了嗎？ ^^

✅ 怕死 "I am not ready to die."

我還不想死。聽到這句話我想到一個condom的經典廣告口號 "Slogan"："I will do a lot for love, but I am not ready to die for it." 前面一個句子blah blah blah，然後接I'm not ready to die for it。表達既期待又怕受傷害，又愛又怕。

✅ 窒息 "smothering"

窒息的，這個字也常用在感情關係中，比如讓人喘不過氣的愛 "Smothering love"，社會新聞上充斥著以愛為名的偏差行為 "Deviance ['dɪ•vɪəns]"。順便背這句愛之深責之切 "Tough love"。愛情愛情，多少罪惡假汝之名 "Oh Love, love, how many crimes are committed in the name."

喔，你會讓我窒息的，離我遠點。

Whoa! You are smothering me, and I need my space.

—— 《Family Guy 09x18 Its A Trap》

他會找到一個喜歡他那種管緊緊的人。

He'll find someone that appreciates his kind of smothering love.

—— 《*Girls 01x05*》

他給我們加罰了泡在冷水裡四個小時，直到天亮才從水裡爬出來。愛之深責之切嘛。

He gave us five extra hours of cold-water conditioning. We didn't get out of the water till dawn. That's tough love for you.

—— 《*Hawaii Five O 01x07*》

你小時候缺乏母愛，是吧？這叫愛之深責之切，小夥伴。

You weren't held when you were a baby, were you? It's called tough love, partner.

—— 《*Hawaii Five O 01x03*》

雙人高空跳傘 "tandem skydiving"

Tandem是雙人腳踏車，情侶自行車，親子自行車。衍生出雙人座的高空跳傘 "Tandem skydiving"，這樣你就知道為什麼有時候會把參加者 "Participant [pɑr'tɪ•sɪ•pənt]" 叫作乘客Passenger了。

我給你們弄了輛雙人腳踏車。

I got you a tandem bike.

—— 《*How I Met Your Mother 02x03 Brunch*》

ㄟ害 "D'oh"

"Damm it oh!" 的縮寫。美國卡通辛普森家庭中的口頭禪，特別是荷馬‧辛普森他自己幹了件蠢事的時候。可以理解成，fxxk me，我靠，該死，慘了。wiki上有發音，或搜尋影片網站 "The Many D'ohs of Homer Simpson"。

✅ 這張生死狀 "this waiver [wevə-]"

棄權書／免責聲明書 "The waiver and release of liability",安全事項。制式的東西,"Health and safety"。用人話來說,這些東西大概就是些萬一有萬一的話,要你放棄曠日廢時的法律訴訟,面對現實尋求保險援助之類的。

✅ 有大問題就不要參加

如果有以下這些情況您就行行好甭跳了 "We do not recommend that you take a skydive if you are: "

- Been scuba diving in 24 hours——24小時內深潛過的。
- Suffering from spinal or back injury——骨刺、坐骨神經痛,背有問題的(控八空空關心您的健康)。
- Pregnant——孕婦。

✅ 有小問題要告知工作人員

如果您目前就醫中,或有任何情況你覺得跟本次活動安全有關的 "If you're under some medical conditions or any other information we need to know to include you safely in this activity.",就告訴我們

嚴重的暈車暈船、哮喘、過敏、心臟病、羊癇瘋、鼻子不通 "Suffering severe motion sickness, asthma, allergies, heart conditions, epilepsy or suffer from nasal or sinus congestion."

→ 我剛才是說 "I was like…"

我剛才是說…"I have, just said…" 你剛才說到…"You mentioned…"

不好意思，你剛才是說你敲了他的頭？

I'm sorry, did you just say you did conk him on the head?

—— 《Bones 04x05》

我對你稍早說的有些東西蠻感興趣的。

I was interested in some of the things you were saying earlier.

—— 《Bones 04X10》

→ 工作人員 "staff"

這個複數也不加s。

→ 耳鳴 "ears blocked"

Tinnitus [ˈtɪ•nə•təs]。耳壓失衡，耳鳴，坐飛機也很常見，會持續地聽到嗡嗡聲。"Constantly hearing drone"

我有點耳鳴。

I'm getting a little buzzy.

—— 《Cougar Town 1x02》

我剛在那裡嗓子都喊到啞了。他們音樂非得開那麼大嗎？ 我一個字都聽不到，我耳鳴得厲害。

I strained my voice screaming in there. Does it have to be so loud? I can't hear a word. My ears are ringing so bad.

—— 《Friends 04x09 Theyre Going To Party》

✔憋氣 "Hold your breath."

例如 "Hold your nose."

比較 "Don't hold your breath." 除了別憋住氣以外，口語中常用來指：別摒息以待，莫當真勿抱希望別想太多了。

達人提點

✔ 專心聽一下 "Listen up."

聽好了。美國人很多東西會加個up，down什麼的，例如 "Right here, right down here"，加個down感覺很順喔，有些人覺得怎麼老外講起英文就輕鬆自然也沒有用到什麼艱難詞彙 "Big word"，自己講起來就一卡一頓的，善用up，down，over，in這些東西當潤滑劑，會有一定的幫助。

→ 加個 **up**

　Listen, "Listen up."

　Hurry, "Hurry up."

　整理乾淨就馬上走人，clean it and go，再唸下 "Clean it up and go."

→ 同場加映 **right**

　馬上來。你要說Coming也行，加個up怎麼樣，Comin'up，好像厲害一點喔。

　再來個right，唸Comin' right up。噹噹噹～感覺自己從美劇裡走出來了有木有？ ^^

1.4 浪漫夏威夷六天五夜 除了扶桑花還有楊麗花

情境對話

 MP3 004

Danno

怎麼沒有貝殼項鍊接機啦？
Why didn't we get an airport greeting with shell leis?

麥可

花環接機比較好，貝殼放了幾天後聞起來不太妙。
Flower Lei Greetings are better. A few days later shell leis won't smell good.

麥可

跟團很划算，但是花環接機要26美金捏。
The group tour is the best bargain, but it does cost twenty-six dollars.

Danno

聽說楊麗花住在這裡。
I've heard Yang Li-hua lives here.

麥可

嗯啊。
Uh-huh.

麥可

卡哈拉是很高級的住宅區。
Kahala is a very select area.

麥可

到時候在左手邊你可以看到那間著名的豪宅。
On your left, you'll see the famous upscale home.

麥可

楊麗花住在那間黑色屋頂的房子。
Yang Li-hua lives in that house with a black roof.

Danno

我比較好奇電音三太子住在哪裡。
I'm more curious about where SynthPop Nalakuvara stays.

麥可

呃…謝謝你喔…
Er...Mahalo...

Danno

新檀島警騎片頭裡的那個國王銅像…
The King Kamehameha Status which appears in the opening scenes of Hawaii Five-O…

麥可

疑，你看過？！亞歷克斯酷爆了。
Eh, you have seen it?! Alex couldn't get any less cool.

麥可

第五天會去那裡。
On the fifth day, we'll be there.

麥可

你可以看到很多檀島警騎拍片取景的地方。
You'll see lots of film locations for Hawaii Five-O.

Danno

彩虹塔，茉莉亞咖啡…
Rainbow Tower, Cafe Julia…

麥可

歪基基銀行前的那場槍戰場景。
A shootout scene right in front of Bank of Waikiki.

Danno

我是葛蕾絲朴的超級粉絲 :D。
I'm a huge fan of Grace Park :D.

Danno

四十歲保養得真好。她真是凍齡。
She is looking really great for 40. She's ageless.

麥可

其實她不是我的菜，但是她有一種魅力…
Actually, she is not my cup of tea, but her charm works in a way…

Danno
對，搞不清楚，你就是有一種～一種說不上來的…
Yeah, I-I don't know, you just have a-a...

Vivien
咳咳，你們男生對動作片還真是有興趣是吧。
Ahem, you guys are really interested in some action huh.

Danno
不然你想聊侏儸紀公園嗎？
Or you wanna talk about Jurassic Park?

麥可
我們也會去著名的古蘭尼牧場，侏儸紀公園的拍攝場地。
We'll also visit the famous Kualoa Ranch, which was the filming site for Jurassic Park.

Vivien
…
…

Danno
我覺得冷場了。
I'm sensing a lull.

麥可
順便提一下，這裡的海灘婚禮吊炸天。
BTW, the Kahala ocean wedding will blow you away.

Danno
冷場，嘿嘿。
Lull, hehe.

麥可
阿拉摸阿娜購物中心，打三折。
Ala Moana Center, seventy percent discount.

Vivien
什麼時候去！？
When!?

麥可
明天。
Tomorrow ^^".

☆ 單詞與句型

✔ 扶桑花 "Hibiscus"；楊麗花 "Yang Li-hua"

Hibiscus [haɪ'bɪs•kəs]，夏威夷草裙舞女郎頭上戴的就是這種花。

我謹代表我們神奇的瑟牟恩火舞者和大溪地草裙舞女郎向各位致謝。現在夏威夷古早味的朱蕉葉烤豬八戒終於要開窯了。

Thank you on behalf of our amazing Samoan Fire Dancers and our Tahitian Hula Girls. Now it's finally time to unearth the traditional Kalua Pig.

—— 《*Hawaii Five O 01x08*》

✔ 聞起來不太妙 "Won't smell good."

比較 Smell funny，貶義詞。不是聞起來很好笑，是聞起來怪怪的不對勁，常指食物壞掉的味道。

雷，你聞下這味道是不是怪怪的？

Ray, does this smell funny to you?

—— 《*Everybody Loves Raymond 01x05 Look Don't Touch*》

美國清涼油弄得我手上聞起來很奇怪。

Vaporub makes my hands smell funny.

—— 《*The Big Bang 01x11*》

→ 引申的用法

我聞到艾美獎的味道。

I smell an Emmy (Emmy Award.)

—— 《*2 Broke Girls 02x22*》

聞起來很有異國風。

That smells exotic.

—— 《Bobs Burgers 01x04》

哦我不知道但是⋯聞上去有加勒比海的味道！

Oh, I don't know, but...smells Caribbean to me [kæ'rɪ•bɪən]!

—— 《Everybody Hates Chris 02x18》

✔高級住宅區 "a very select area"；豪宅 "upscale home"

形容高級常用的字有 "Exclusive / upscale / luxury / expensive" 住宅區則是後面加上 "Residence / residential area / residential district." 例如 他們住在高級住宅區 "They live a posh part of town."

比較 貧民區 "slum / glade / ghetto ['gɛto]"

他從前住在貧民區。

Yeah, he's been in a slum.

—— 《Everybody Loves Raymond 04x03 You Bet》

我沒料到，貧民區竟會滿地機關槍。

I didn't count on the possibility that the glades could be flooded with machine guns.

—— 《Arrow 01x05》

你要跳脫你的魯蛇心態。

You need to rise above your ghetto mentality [mɛn'tæ•lə•tɪ].

—— 《Everybody Hates Chris 02x02》

✅ 片頭 "the opening scenes"

例如 the opening credits。

有頭的就是Opening，主題則是Theme；有音樂沒歌詞的，music，有歌詞的，song。所以主題曲，主題音樂怎麼說呢？"Theme music"。片頭主題歌就是 "Opening Theme Song" 囉。

我以前害怕美劇派瑞・梅森的片頭。

I used to be scared of the opening credits to Perry Mason.

—— 《*Everybody Hates Chris 02x11*》

✅ 保養 "looking great"

關於身體外在保養的好最簡單的就是說 "Keep herself up, keep herself fit"，反之可以用 "She has drooped."

她保養的真不錯。

She really keeping herself up.

—— 《*Shameless Us 01x10*》

我的身材是不是垮了？ 我沒感覺。別說了，黛布，你看起來很美。

Have I drooped? I wouldn't know about that. Stop it, Deb, you look great.

—— 《*Everybody Loves Raymond 09x14*》

他不懂得好好保養身體，淨吃些個垃圾食品又酗酒。

He never took care of himself, ate like crap, and drank too much.

—— 《*Modern Family 01x23*》

→ 其他關於保養得很好 "in good nick / well-maintained"
（ 比較 車輛的定期保養 "regular maintenance" ）

這雙運動鞋的狀況保養的很好，只是鞋底磨光了。

The trainers are in good nick, except the sole has been well worn.

—— 《Sherlock 01x03》

你們有沒有注意到那棟政府大樓保養的相當好？

Did you ever notice how the government buildings there are quite well-maintained?

—— 《Family Guy 09X15 Brothers & Sisters》

✔ 看過 "have seen"

去電影院看用 "See"，但電視用 "Watch"，比較值得注意的一點是，看電影用 "Go to the movies" 就可以了，不用go to see the movie。

你們看過《軍官與紳士》嗎？

Did you ever see 《An Officer and a Gentleman》?

—— 《Friends 01X10》

看過逃獄驚魂嗎？

Have you ever seen the film 《The Defiant Ones》?

—— 《Everybody Hates Chris 02x06》

喂，我看過所有的007電影。

Look, I've seen all the Bond films.

—— 《Femme Fatales 01x04》

我攤牌了，我從來沒看過那片子。

Cards on the table. I never saw the movie.

—— 《Be Wtih You 01X16》

✓ 的超級粉絲 "a huge fan of"

見到你我太激動了，我侄女是你的超級粉絲。

Hi. What a thrill to meet you. My niece is a big fan of yours.

—— 《Hannah Montana She's A Super Sneak-Hibocbii》

克里斯，我知道你一定是Ernie Hudson的大粉絲。

Chris, I know you must be a big Ernie Hudson fan.

—— 《Everybody Hates Chris 02X15》

我可是你的頭號粉絲。

I'm your number one fan.

—— 《Femme Fatales 01x01》

✓ 拍片取景的地方 "Filming Locations"

數不清的電視電影都在夏威夷取景，比如侏儸紀公園《Jurassic Park》，迷失《Lost》，貓王的藍色夏威夷《Blue Hawaii》，喜歡檀島警騎的上網搜尋Five-0 Undercover就可以看到很多主要場景（Major scenes）第幾季第幾集在哪裡拍的。美劇迷如果出發前做點功課，到時候玩起來會更加的處處是驚喜喔 :D

我已經說服伍迪艾倫來克利夫蘭拍片了，就在我們繁華的迪克西蘭爵士片場取景。

I convinced Woody to shoot here in Cleveland, based on our thriving Dixieland Jazz scene.

—— 《Hot In Cleveland 04x01 That Changes Everything》

✔ 動作片 "action"

動作片或喜劇你比較喜歡哪一個？動作片。

Action or comedy? Action.

—— 《Friends 05X22 The One With Joeys Big Break》

我喜歡浪漫喜劇勝過於動作片。

I like rom-coms more than action movies (romantic comedies.)

—— 《Franklin And Bash 02x06》

✔ 古蘭尼牧場 "KUALOA Ranch"

KUALOA is pronounced Koo-ah-low-ah，念作：哭啊捜啊。

✔ 冷場 "lull"

你照顧艾美讓我來處理冷場。

You take care of Amy and I'll take care of the lull.

—— 《Everybody Loves Raymond 07X21 The Shower》

你講了個你認為會很好笑的故事。可是…沒人笑。 所以你在怨嘆我在派對裡是個冷場帝？

You told a story that you thought was gonna be funny. But it...nobody laughed. So you regret that I'm a stiff at parties?

—— 《Everybody Loves Raymond 05x07 The Walk To The Door》

☑ 護照與酒

酒的話可以在某些海灘邊的酒吧小酌，但是不能拿個啤酒瓶在海灘晃來晃去。還有就是老外看亞洲人只要是瘦的就想說是年紀輕，所以不管你是不是娃娃臉，最好隨身帶著護照，以備萬一服務人員需要你出示證件時不至敗興而歸。

護照，麻煩一下？

Pass, please?

―― 《Sherlock 02x02 The Hounds Of Baskerville》

☑ 菸的規定很嚴

06年就已頒布禁菸法案，14年更擴大範圍，大部分地方都不能抽就對了。左顧右盼沒警察？海灘上的救生員同時也身負執法的責任。雖說旅館裡法令規定百分之20的客房可以作為不禁菸客房，但是有些旅館並沒有設置此種客房，而是全館禁菸。罰金也很高，第一次罰款100美金，第二次以後為500美金，抽根菸的罰款都快可以參加韓國購物團6日遊了。關於當地菸酒的規定要特別注意，通常旅行社也都會在行程表或電話說明會中提醒旅客。

☑ 退房注意

歐美國家是約定成俗要付小費的，不習慣的人可以試著把付小費跟說謝謝連在一起，特別是美國。餐館裡忘了給小費就走了，服務生會追出來，問你哪裡不滿意？每天早上離開酒店前記得在枕頭放上至少一塊美金，現金不要隨便丟在房間內，以免被當作小費收走。重要物品統一放在保險櫃 ^^。

1.5

瘋旅遊
德國法蘭克福成人秀

💬 情境對話

 MP3 005

TED

這裡有點吵，裡面還好吧？
It's a little loud in here. Is everything all right in there?

麥可

沒事妥妥滴。
We are good.

TED

現在我們怎麼進去？
Now how are we gonna get in there?

麥可

跟我走。
Come with me.

麥可

店家退我們兩塊抵用券，等她們跳完舞你再發小費，免得給過之後有些又來要一次。
We got a coupon for two dollars off. You can tip the girls after the show, in case some might ask you to tip them twice.

麥可

你也可以上去一起玩喔。
You can join them.

TED

怎麼玩？
How?

麥可

把小費夾在耳朵上，轉過去，還有這裡這裡跟那裡那裡。
Put those bills in your ear, turn around, and here and there.

哈哈哈，額滴神啊！
Hahaha, oh my!

你看那女狼隨著崔斯艾金斯的音樂聲響起，跳著舞到處送飛吻。
（搜Trace Adkins Honky Tonk Badonkadonk）
You see the girls of Coyote Ugly. They blow kisses while dancing to Trace Adkin's "Badonkadonk dance."

The crowds
再大點聲～（Badonkadonk歌詞裡的第一句口白）
Turn it up some~

面朝上躺在舞台，精彩的就來了。泰德上上上！
Now that's heaven right there on the stage, this is the best part, TED. Go Go Go!

她們朝我爬過來用嘴巴叼走小費，有一個好像是男的。
They crawled toward me, and took the tips away with their teeth. One of them was a guy or something.

那是男舞者，他們超級火辣。
That was a Danseur [dɑn'sɝ]. They are super-duper sexy.

這裡開始熱鬧了，啊～啊啊！他們把椅子拿出來了，這是要鬧哪樣？
Now we got a little shindig here. Aaah~ Ah ah! They've got a chair, and what's going on in there?

Party people
給我們更多的這抒情爵士吧！
Let's crank up the smooth jazz!

明天我們還在這裡。今晚就玩到這裡吧。
We'll stay at the same hotel tomorrow. Let's call it a night.

好，結束了走了。
OK, over and out.

TED 疑？那家是什麼？
Eh? What is that?

麥可 兩小時玩到飽的。每個房間門口都有個小窗，先看看再決定要不要進去。
Two hours for all you can play. There's a peephole on the room door, take a look before you knock on the door.

麥可 進去房間後過每半個小時也可以換別間。
You can do some room-switching fun after half an hour.

TED 這附近有沒有7-11？
Are there any 7-elevens around here?

麥可 德國沒有7-11。我們看看車站裡有什麼可以買吧。
We don't have it in Germany. Let's try the station.

麥可 等下，別急著往前走，回頭看一下柱子旁那人。
Hold on, slow down, turn around and check the one next to pillar.

麥可 法蘭克福車站的特警很帥喔。
The SWAT in Frankfurt railway station is pretty cool.

麥可 他的眼睛像雷達似的左右掃描。
Scanning his eyes side to side like a radar.

麥可 身體往前傾斜10度。感覺隨時會如暴風般衝出去的樣子。
Leaning forward at a 10-degree angle. It's like he'll have to storm out in any time.

TED 真的耶！霸氣側漏五月天！
So true! He couldn't get any less cool!

☆ 單詞與句型

✔ 如暴風般衝出去 "to storm out"

迅雷不及掩耳的速度，閃電般的速度，暴風旋風疾風般的速度，用光電風雷這類咚咚形容速度在中英文裡都很常見，以下請看 "To rush out／to rush in"的例句：

我們為什麼要急著離開？

Why'd we rush out so fast?

—— 《*Friends 07x18 Joey's Award*》

他們叫我放下手頭所有的事趕過來這裡，就為這個。

Oh, that's why they told me to drop everything and rush in here.

—— 《*Homeland 01x08*》

我們的意思是，不要操之過急。

All we're saying is, don't rush into anything.

—— 《*Friends 03x18 The Hypnosis Tape*》

✔ 跟我走 "I am the door way."

我帶路，我熟門熟路，跟我走就對了。除了耳熟能詳的雷磁狗 "Let's go" 跟花樓咪 "Follow me"，"Come with me" 你可以跟 "Walk with me" 比較感覺一下。

你，跟我來。

You, come with me.

—— 《*Cougar Town 2x15*》

天終於晴了。陪我走走吧。

The sun is finally shining. Come walk with me.

—— 《Game Of Thrones 01x02》

✔ 雷達 "radar"

除了實體的雷達，也有其他各種引申的用法，比如在美劇《Franklin And Bash》中出現的：我們可不像你一樣，配備了軍用級別的同性戀檢測儀 "Well, we're not all blessed with your military-grade gaydar." 還有在《Modern Family》中出現的：我來是想告訴你，你的基達壞掉了，細漢仔不是同性戀 "I'm here to let you know your gaydar is broken, shorty is not gay."

好的，紅外線雷達顯示裡面有個人。

All right, FLIR scan shows people inside.

—— 《Hawaii Five O 03x07》

我可以真切的感受到他們不希望我在場。知道嗎，我有這方面的雷達。

And I could really sense that they didn't want me there. You know, I have a radar for stuff like that.

—— 《Cougar Town 1x24》

✔ 舞台 "stage"

大家噓他下台。

Everyone booed him off the stage.

—— 《Friends 09x13 Where Monica Sings》

✅ 開始熱鬧了 "Got a little shindig [ˈʃɪndɪg]."

你們準備好要熱鬧下了嗎？
Are you guys ready to make some noise?

—— 《Girls 01x06》

這地方有的熱鬧了。
This thing's going to rock.

—— 《Everybody Loves Raymond 05x08 Young Girl》

這兒很熱鬧啊，唷！
And this place is ragin', yo! (ragin'=raging)

—— 《How I Met Your Mother 04x13 Three Days Of Snow》

好吧。被你抓到了。我就是喜歡熱鬧。
Fine. You got me. I like to be around people.

—— 《Cougar Town 1x07》

✅ 朝我爬過來 "crawl toward me"

爬過來，蹲下身子！
And crawl over here, and stay low!

—— 《2 Broke Girls 02X12》

還有跟Crawl for it躡手躡腳的過來，可以比較聯想一下一起記的。

有兩個穿長袍的人，從我們的九點鐘方向一路躡手躡腳的過來。
Looks like two men in black pajamas, creeping along at our nine o'clock.

—— 《Generation Kill 01x03 Screwby》

上上上！ "Go go go!"

翻成去去去？感覺上上上比較有那gogogo的Fu，另外也常用 "Good to go"，跟 "Ready to go" 意思一樣的。

我把工具箱放在外面，所有要用的東西都準備好了，我想我們可以出發了！

I laid the toolbox outside, and all the supplies are ready, and I think we are good to go!

—— 《Modern Family 02x01》

你們到哪裡了，兄弟？我們準備好可以出發了，老大。

Where are we at, guys? We are good to go, boss.

好的，我數一二三就行動。

All right, you move in on my mark.

—— 《Person Of Interest 01x23》

待我一聲令下就分離反應堆，3…2…1…分離。

Reactor-module separation on my mark. Three, two, one, mark.

—— 《Stargate 06x20 Memento》

目標B正在向你那邊移動。20英尺…10英尺…準備。開火！

B Target moving towards you. 20 feet…ten feet…On my mark. Now!

—— 《24Hrs 08x16》

響起 "while dancing to"

英文裡各種表達響起的方法。

➜ 音樂響起

沒有甜蜜的獨立搖滾歌曲響起。

No sweet indie rock song that swells up. (Independent rock)

—— 《*How I Met Your Mother 03x01 Wait For It*》

羅密歐與茱麗葉的愛情主題曲響起。

Romeo & juliet love theme plays.

—— 《*Coupling 1x02 Size Matters*》

每次李察‧基爾開車去接黛博拉‧溫姬我都會哭。當他帶她出去時。片子就響起喬‧庫克的歌？（想聽這首歌的搜尋**Up Where We Belong**）

I cry every time Richard Gere picks up Debra Winger. And he carries her out, and that Joe Cocker song comes on?

—— 《*Franklin And Bash 02x07*》

➜ 腦海中響起

當時我的頭腦中好像響起了《陰陽魔界》的主題曲。

I had this little theme from 《*Twilight Zone*》 go off in my head "ner-ner-ner-ner..."

—— 《*The Secret 2006*》

➜ 其他響起

當警報響起的時候我還在吃飯。

I was still at chow when the alarm went off.

—— 《*Stargate 07x16 Death Knell*》

我記得有一次除夕夜派對，午夜鐘聲響起時，他向我擊掌了。

Um, I remember once at a new year's eve party, stroke of midnight, he high-Fived me.

—— 《Modern Family 02x02》

突然響起了槍聲。

Some shots ring out.

—— 《Mad Men 06x07》

（號角聲響起）

(horn call)

—— 《Stargate 04x21 Double Jeopardy》

比賽結束號角聲終於響起，根據Marshall估計，比分是零比零。

When the final horn mercifully blew, the score was, by Marshall's estimate, to nothing.

—— 《How I Met Your Mother 04x19》

✔ 抵用券 "tokens"

代幣，抵用券，賭錢用的籌碼是chips，沒錯就是薯條薯片那個chips。

這些是遊戲幣。

They're game tokens.

—— 《Everybody Hates Chris 02x10》

各位，隨著這次兌換籌碼，我們進入了最後的階段…

Gentlemen, with this chip exchange, we enter the final phase of the game...

—— 《Casino Royale 007》

也可以比如什麼地方發的，就那個地方的名字後面加dollars。

動物園代幣？　是啊，你可以參觀金剛鸚鵡戴帽子表演的小鳥秀。
Zoo dollars? Yes, and come see the bird show at. The macaws wear hats.

—— 《Friends 02x12 The Super Bowl》

達人提點

✅ 看秀

歐洲的旅行團有些會安排看秀，比如法國的紅磨坊 "Moulin rouge"，太陽馬戲團 "Cirque du Soleil"，美國拉斯維加斯的 "Jubilee"，"Mystère by Cirque du Soleil"，這種是沒問題。但是如果在自由活動時間想看點不一樣的，需要配合一下各種地方不同店家五花八門的遊戲規則。

九名隊員打擊，九名隊員守備，這就是遊戲規則。
Nine guys hit, nine guys field, that's the game.

—— 《Everybody Loves Raymond 03x07 Moving Out》

✅ 越夜越美麗

店雖然龍蛇混雜，不就花錢湊熱鬧嘛，說多了記不住，在此講兩個不能不注意的重點：其一是忌諱裝內行不照當時當地的遊戲規則走，其二是5字箴言，別貪小便宜，常出問題的都是這種。貪小便宜通常不是錢的問題，而是犯了癮戒不掉。盡量自己保持好心情。

他就愛貪小便宜。
He's a bargain drinker.

—— 《Shameless Us 02x08》

1.6

瘋旅遊 德國深度10日夢幻新天鵝 堡、波登湖賞美景

💬 情境對話

 MP3 006

Rebekah

我想幫我們拍合照，可是我沒帶相機。
I wanted to take our picture, but I didn't have my camera.

麥可

我去拿我的照相機。
I'll go get my camera.

Rebekah

麥可，你的照相機準備好了嗎？
Michael, is your camera ready?

Rebekah

這裡，幫我們拍合照。
Here, take our picture.

麥可

好，轉過來看這裡。
Turn and face the camera.

Rebekah

這樣就好了。別拍我的左臉。我的痘痘越來越大顆了。
This is it. I don't wanna show the left side of my face. My pimple's getting worse.

麥可

感謝風的降臨，我們可以拍到美女的走光照囉～
Thank you dear wind. Here comes the up-skirt photo~

Rebekah

什麼跟什麼啦…你個流氓（噗）
What the... You're an asshole *Chuckle*

麥可
而你很靚。好了。
And you're beautiful. Done.

Rebekah
我看看,讓我看看。
Show me. Let me see that.

Rebekah
根本沒拍清楚。
That's just a blur.

麥可
再拍一次?
One more time?

Rebekah
再拍一次,拜託了。盡量多拍幾張。
One more, please. Take as many photos as possible.

Rebekah
現在我想拍獨照。
Now, I want a shot of myself alone.

Rebekah
你可以把這些照片傳上網,或寄給我嗎?
Could you just put these photos online or mail them to me?

麥可
沒問題,來笑一個,你上鏡頭了。
Sure. Smile. You're on Camera.

Rebekah
你拍了嗎?
Did you get that on camera?

麥可
好了。你來看看,好多張。
Okay. Come take a look. A lot of pictures.

Rebekah
這張拍的不錯。
This is a great shot.

Rebekah
這特寫拍的好讚,這一張也拍的很好。
A nice close-up. That's another good one.

停，這裡。這照片是在哪裡拍的？
Stop. There. Where was this photo taken?

在法蘭克福拍的。
That one was shot at Frankfurt.

照片裡右邊的人是你…那這張呢？
And this is you in this photo on the right… How about this one?

這張拍的是波登湖。我從陽台上拍的。
This one is Bodensee. I took that right from the balcony.

美呆了，太夢幻了。
Awesome, unreal.

跟我說說這張照片的故事。
What can you tell me about this picture?

什麼故事？為什麼一定要有個故事？
What story? Why should there be a story?

每個人過去都有不同的故事。講個故事對你來說還不是信手拈來。
Well, we were all something else once upon a time. To make up a story, it would be as easy as snapping your fingers.

別再相信沒有根據的說法了。
Stop believing in a nonsense with no proof.

故事。快說。
Story. Go.

☆ 單詞與句型

✓ 笑一個 "smile"

笑一個，最常見的就是say cheeze，但是是這樣說，恩，笑起來不自然，cheeze這個字事實上讓嘴巴張開的的很不自然 "The word cheese actually stretches your mouth into an unnatural."

微笑說Everyday～或大笑說MOCHA，一些尾音發「ㄟ」或「啊」音的字 "Say words that end in uh"，讓嘴角自然上揚 "To bring the corners of the mouth up naturally"，這類用語也有各種無厘頭的說法試著把人真的逗笑，那是最自然的了。

✓ 拍合照 "take our picture"

picture有照片，也有圖片，畫的意思。拍照在旅遊中可以說是家常便飯，我們現在用例句——來把picture的用法練到流利起來。先說最熟悉的用 "Take pictures"：

我可不能穿著這身衣服照相。
I can't take my pictures in this.
　　——《Everybody Hates Chris 1x13 Everybody Hates Picture Day》

你想幹嘛？你打算穿這個拍照？
What are you doing? You're taking the picture dressed like that?
　　——《Everybody Loves Raymond 04x11 The Christmas Picture》

我要幫你拍照。
I get to take pictures of you.
　　——《Cougar Town 1x17》

✅ 拍照／照片 "snap / shot"

隨便拍幾張 "Take some snaps"，隨便拍張 "Snap a shot"。一張快照 "A snapshot" 是不慢慢調整構圖與光圈，你就拍拍拍拍拍就對了，然後挑幾張好看的，其他不喜歡的就刪刪刪刪刪。抓的是自然的那一瞬間 "Stolen moment"，反正現在都是數位相機，底片不花錢。大頭照 "Head shot / resume shot"，警局檔案照 "Mug shot"。另外順便記一下數碼相機 "Digital camera"，拍立得照相機 "Polaroid ['poˑləˌrɔɪd] camera"。之前資料備份沒搞好，很多照片都不見了。整理了一部分給大家參考，可以邊看看照片邊讀英語更有Fu，至於照片在哪裡？答案就在本書中，有看完的人就自然會找到喔 ^^。

露西，讓我照一張。 不行，你在那裏別動。我來照。
Lucy, let me get a shot. No, you stay there. I want to take it.

——《The Pacific 08》

你能不能幫我個忙拍張照片？
Could you do me a favor and just snap a shot?

——《Franklin And Bash 02x04》

✅ 自拍 "selfie"

自從有手機有了照相功能跟facebook後，女生們除了照鏡子以外，又多了一個自拍的樂趣。這個字也成了牛津詞典的年度風雲詞彙。比較 自拍影片 "Home tape"。

史上最爛的自拍照，是不？
Worst selfie ever, right?

——《2 Broke Girls 02x21》

不要帶手機，婚禮上別搞自拍。今天要關注的是新娘的美而不是你自己。

No phones. No…no…no wedding selfies. Today's about focusing on a beauty other than your own.

—— 《Selfie 01x01》

現在已經設定好，可以拍了。按下錄影鍵就行。加了個油。

Now, you're all set up, good to go. Just hit record. Good luck.

—— 《Friends 08x04 The Videotape》

✔ 拍下來了 "photographed"；錄下來了 "videotaped"

存證可以用"Document"。**例如** 我可得保留證據 "I gotta document this."
另外常說的一句，沒圖沒真相 "Pics or it didn't happen."

警方會拍照取證的。

The police would have photographed ['fo•tə•græft].

—— 《Arrow 01x06 Legacies》

但我有義務告訴你，這次的面試有錄影存證。

But I feel obligated to tell you that this meeting is being videotaped.

—— 《Friends 05x17 The One With Rachel's Inadvertent Kiss》

→ 把電視節目錄下來：**DVR'd**

節目結束了，但我錄下來了。

The show's over, but I dvr'd it.

—— 《Cougar Town 1x18》

In the picture

picture有照片，也有圖片，畫的意思。所以in the picture，也有在照片中或畫中兩種意思。

→ 在照片中。

我們要拍第一張室友合照，對。要不你也一起來拍吧？
We're about to take our first ever roommate picture. Yeah. Hey, why don't you get in the picture, too?
—— 《How I Met Your Mother 05x18 Say Cheese》

你的朋友，照片中的那個人。
Your friend, the one in the picture.
—— 《Prison Break 03x03 Call Waiting》

照片裡站在你旁邊的是誰？
Who's that in the picture with you?
—— 《The Air I Breathe》

你還說不想在照片裡顯胖。
You also said you didn't want to look fat in the pictures.
—— 《Be Wtih You 01x22》

→ 在一幅畫中。

羅伯特伯伯，我給你畫了幅畫。還有我把媽咪也畫進去了。
I drew a picture of you, uncle Robert. And that's Mommy in the picture, too.
—— 《Everybody Loves Raymond 07x04 Pet The Bunny》

✅Not in the picture.

除了原義不在照片中的意思，另有引申這人不在了，比如離開了跑了，
不存在，沒資料。

他們的父母呢？父不詳。

What happened to the parents? No father in the picture.

—— 《*Person Of Interest 01x14*》

✅拍了 "Get that on camera."

拍到。拍到了嗎？有拍到嗎？剛才有飛碟耶，你拍到了嗎？ ^^

你剛剛相機拍下了嗎？拍到了。

Did we get that on camera? Right on camera.

—— 《*Femme Fatales 01x07*》

✅信手拈來 "As easy as snapping your fingers."

舉手之勞，不費彈指之力，不費吹灰之力，也可以說 "As easy as a
snap"，"As easy as falling of a log"，"As easy as ABC"。或直接說 "It's
a snap."

這就跟數123一樣簡單。

It's as easy as one, two, three.

—— 《*Hot In Cleveland 04x07 Magic Diet Candy*》

用這些隨手可得的中國食材做菜，就跟叫外賣一樣簡單。

Cooking with these readily available Chinese ingredients is as easy
as ordering from a takeaway.

—— 《*Chinese Food Made Easy 01x00*》

不那麼簡單呢？

例如 歹誌不是像憨人所想的安捏 "It's not as easy as you had thought."

並且我跟你們保證這沒有你們所想的那麼容易。

And I can guarantee you it won't be as easy as you think.

—— 《*Stargate 07x07 Enemy Mine*》

開這鎖有點小麻煩，瑞斯先生。這沒有看起來那麼簡單。

Little trouble picking this lock, Mr. Reese. It's not as easy as it looks.

—— 《*Person Of Interest 01x06*》

要負責管理可沒有聽起來的那麼簡單。

Taking charge wasn't as easy as it sounded.

—— 《*Everybody Hates Chris 02x02*》

達人提點

不准拍照 "No pictures."

有些地方比如賣衣服的怕款式被山寨，有的是擔心打開閃光燈 "Activate the flash-lamp" 會傷害展品，還有的是不想你一直拍照沒有專心看表演，或閃光燈影響了別人看表演 "Affecting people with the flash"，各種原因都有可能，一般都會在門口有貼紙或警語。

→ 日本拍照

路邊的攤販上的食材，問一下多半會給拍的。老公上班去了，兩個年輕媽媽在公園聊天，一旁睡在腳踏車裡可愛的嬰兒能不能拍？也是要問一下，有的不喜歡孩子被拍臉，怕被綁架什麼的不知道。畢竟是陌生人嘛，反正就都問一下就對了。

➔ 關於導遊應該穿什麼衣服

第一天穿長褲，正式一點，有些公司規定不要穿牛仔褲。然後就看是帶客人去什麼地方，這個不死板，因時因地制宜唄 "Well, that depends."

說實話，我不知道，我忘了上次導遊穿什麼。上班時是不是要穿西裝？天啊，夏天你會熱死。
TBH, IDK. I don't remember what the tour guides wore. Do you have to suit up when you are on duty? Geez you'd die, in hot weather.
比較 TBH"to be honest,"IDK"I donno, I don't know."

我無法想像在大熱天裡穿西裝，在海灘上穿？
I can't imagine wearing suit in hot climes, on the beach?

我從沒想到你是個這麼死板固執的人。
I never would have taken you for such a stickler.

—— 《*Mad Men 06x07*》

你們死板又毫無幽默感。
You are rigid and humorless.

—— 《*Bones 04X12*》

PART 2
東北亞超值體驗

2.1 日本嚴選 新宿歌舞伎町、偶像握手秀

💬 情境對話

MP3 007

麥可

等一下過馬路以後，請先不要拍照。看完秀以後會有時間可以拍的。
After we cross the street, no pictures please. You will have your time to take some photos after the show.

麥可

不管誰跟你講話，都別看他。
No matter who talks to you, don't look at them.

志村けん

我看見那邊有人在發傳單。
I see someone is passing out flyers there.

麥可

給你傳單或什麼名片都別拿，請勿脫隊喔。
Don't take flyers or any cards, and don't fall behind please.

麥可

等一下我們開始走的時候，記得在到那裡之前不要停下腳步。
Remember when we move, do not stop until we get in there.

麥可

這裡有一家便利店，有人要帶零食進去嗎？
There's a convenient store here. Anyone wanna bring some snacks in?

志村けん

我其實剛吃了麥香雞。
I actually just had some McChicken.

好，那我們走了。
K, then we move on.

麥可，你知道我是外貌協會的。
Michael, you know I like to play shallow douchebag's game.

逆砍砍，那家看起來不錯。
Psst, that one looks good.

那家是偽娘秀，人妖酒吧。
That's a drag queen show, okama Bar.

我剛才說的話收回。
I take it back.

如果還有時間也可以安排。（壞笑）
It could be arranged if we still have time. *evil grin*

嗯好，臉紅心跳的時間到了！在此簡單說明一下。
All right, time to be bad! Break it down for me.

一位舞者會放三首歌。
They will play three songs during each dancer's show.

現場不能用自己的相機或手機拍照喔。
No pictures with your own camera or cell here.

如果想要拍照留念的話。
Unless you want to take a picture for a souvenir.

她的舞跳完後，她會提一個花籃出來謝幕，然後花籃裡有一個拍立得，拍一張500日幣。
After the show, she will take a curtain call with a picnic basket, and there's a Polaroid in the basket, one photo for 500 Yen.

然後握個手。
And shake your hand.

隨時可以出來外面這裡抽菸或上廁所，但是請不要上樓走出門口。
You can come out anytime to smoke here or take a bio-break, but please don't go upstairs and walk out of that door.

那如果等一下我餓了呢？
What if I get hungry later?

你去便利店弄點東西吃。
You go grab some food from 7-Eleven.

當天出入都只算一次錢，但是出去前要拿張出入證。
They won't charge you twice on the same day, but before you go out you need to get a re-entry ticket.

我說的餓不是肚子餓的餓。
I'm not talking about being hungry for food.

這個…玩雞同鴨講嗎？
Well... Am I in a different conversation?

你明明知道我說的是什麼意思。
You know what I mean.

缺愛嗎？有一天你會遇到你的夢中情人的。
Hungry for love? Some day you'll find your cuttie pie.

還有問題嗎？
Any questions?

要是我流鼻血怎麼辦？
What if I got the nosebleeds?

麥可

廁所裡有衛生紙，志村健你最調皮了，麥擱鬧啊～
You can use the toilet paper in the rest room. Bad bad Shimura Ken, knock it off~

☆ 單詞與句型

✓ 外貌協會 "shallow douchebag's game"

我是欣賞漂亮女人，但並沒有得了七仔癌。

I admire hotties, but I don't play shallow douchebag's game.

—— 《倚天屠龍記之張無忌他娘說得對》

我不是外貌協會。

Well, I don't like to judge a book by its cover.

—— 《2 Broke Girls 1x14 Proper And The Upstairs Neighbor》

✓ 偽娘秀 "drag queen show"

例如 變裝癖者 "A cross dresser / transvestite [træns'ves•taɪt]"。比較 變性者 "a ladyboy / a transsexual [træn'sɛk•ʃʊəl]."

我化的妝比偽娘還濃。

I'm wearing more makeup than a drag queen.

—— 《Everybody Loves Raymond 04x05 The Will》

泰德，在網上騷擾男人的美女，要不是瘋子，妓女要不就是偽娘。

Ted, the only hot girls that troll the internet for dudes are crazy, hookers, or dude.

—— 《How I Met Your Mother 03x05 How I Met Everyone Else》

是啊，我會坐在採購部那個人妖旁邊。

Sure. I'll just sit next to the transsexual from purchasing.

—— 《*Friends 03x21 A Chick And A Duck*》

✅ 花籃 "basket / a picnic basket"

野餐手提籃，藤編手提籃，講到籃子就想到籃球 "basketball" 是吧，還有放髒衣服的洗衣籃 "a laundry basket"，垃圾桶除了trash can，也說the wastebasket。我們常說的雞蛋不能放在一個籃子裡，要多角化經營 "You got to diversify [dɪ'və•sə•faɪ]. "A basket case就比較難聯想，這是形容一個人只能窩在籃子裡讓人家把他抬來抬去，引申為這人撿角了，沒救了。下面的例句用來形容有些男生只要見到女人就走不動路渾然忘我咚吱咚吱的。

你們這些男人都怎麼回事？為什麼當你們看見一個女孩…這人就變得無藥可救了？

What is it with you guys? Why is it when one of you sees a girl... He becomes a basket case?

—— 《*Everybody Loves Raymond 01x05 Look Don't Touch*》

✅ 出入證 "a free pass ticket"

日常生活中各式各樣的通行證，出入證。最簡單的你就記pass，**例如** 出示你的通行證！"I need to see your pass!"。site pass則可以用於現實生活中的某個站點，或網站也行。

抱歉，沒有通行證誰也進不去。

Uh, sorry, nobody gets in here without a site pass.

—— 《*Howimym 07x05*》

✅ 通行證 "clearance [k'lɪ•rəns]"

clearance是放行，通關的意思。海關準行／結關 "Customs Clearance"。另申請到某些地區旅遊、移民時要準備的良民證是Police Clearance Certificate [sə'tɪ•fɪ•kət]。

恢復瑞德小姐的通行證。
Just reinstate Ms. Reed's clearance now.

—— 《24Hrs 08x02》

我的安檢出入證已經被吊銷了。
My security clearance has been revoked.

—— 《Batman Begins 2005》

✅ 停車場出入管制卡，感應卡

一張你們停車場出入管制卡在一位叫加爾•沃倫的死者的公寓被發現。
One of your parking lot access cards. Was found in the apartment of a victim, cal Warren.

—— 《Bones 04x11》

那是一張停車場通行證健身中心的。
Turns out it was a parking lot entrance ticket from the Rec Center (Recreation Center [ˌrɛkrɪ'eʃən].)

—— 《Hawaii Five O 03x18》

司機，這是停車場通行證。
Driver, here's the parking pass.

—— 《Cat Run》

其他通行証如：

放風通行證 "hall pass"，有部限制級喜劇電影就叫Hall Pass，討論男女雙方婚後可不可以擁有自己的「那種」私人空間，無厘頭很搞笑，中文譯名：放風通行證／偷情許可証／嘿咻卡。

還呆在走廊的學生必須有放風通行証。

Any student out in the hall has to have a hall pass.

—— 《Everybody Hates Chris 02x12》

後台通行證，快走。

Backstage pass. Let's go.

—— 《Howimym 08x18》

雞同鴨講 "Am I in a different conversation?"

狀況外，我out了嗎？我們跑題了 "We're getting off-topic here."

你跑題啦，拉回正題。

You're going off-point. Bring it back.

—— 《Be Wtih You 01x09》

有點跑題了吧，大哥。

It's a bit off-topic, sir.

—— 《Franklin And Bash 02x09》

是的，嗯，完全穿越了。

Yes, well, that's neither here nor there.

—— 《Friends 05x13 The One With Joeys Bag》

好了，我們講正題。

Ok, let's try to stay on topic.

—— 《*Modern Family 01x18*》

✔ 謝幕 "take a curtain call"

或許我應該退休。優雅的一鞠躬謝幕。

Maybe I should retire. Bow out gracefully.

—— 《*Hustle 01x06 The Last Gamblemafriki*》

我覺得你表現得很好，同時我也覺得你可以見好就收了。

I think you did great, and I think you can take a bow.

—— 《*Hot In Cleveland 04X13 It S Alive*》

✔ 肚子餓 "hungry for food" ；缺愛 "hungry for love"

雙關語，巴尼說 "I'm not talking about hungry for food"，根據後面巴尼提到流鼻血，巴尼當時想表達是 "hungry for sex," 麥可則裝傻把他當做 "hungry for love" 接話，來回答 "Some day you'll find your cuttie pie."

你指的是生理上的飢餓感還是對這份工作的渴求？

Do you mean like physically hungry or hungry for the job?

—— 《*Girls 01x01*》

烤肉就快好了。飢渴的我要的並不是那個烤肉。

The roast is just about ready. That's not what I'm hungry for.

—— 《*American Horror Story 02x01*》

飢不擇食之夜…這些女孩子太渴望得到男性的注意了。

Desperation Night... These girls are so hungry for male attention.

—— 《*How I Met Your Mother 06x16 Desperation Day*》

✅ 麥擱鬧 "knock it off"

別鬧了，別淘氣，鬧夠了吧。類似的說法還有 "drop it / cut it out."

好了，小夥伴們，別鬧了。

Okay, boys, break it up.

— 《2 Broke Girls 1x08 And Hoarder Culture》

鬧夠了吧。不，還沒有，還早著呢。

That's enough of that. No, it's not enough. Not nearly.

— 《Cat Run》

夠了，別鬧了！別鬧了！

Stop it! Cut it out! Cut it out!

— 《Friends 03x21 A Chick And A Duck》

✅ 放我一馬吧／放個水嘛 "cut me some slack"

所以如果你可以的話，麻煩體諒一下我的心情，謝了。說得好，我知道
錯了。

So cut me some slack if you would, please, thank you. Good point.
I'm sorry.

— 《Hawaii Five O 02x14》

👍 達人提點

✅ 廁所 "rest room"

通常行程的安排，每兩個小時讓客人有上洗手間的機會，長途拉車也會

找途中的休息站。廁所在美國一般叫 "rest room, bath room"，或男生的 "men's room"，女生的化妝室 "ladies'room, powder room"，loo也很常見，至於為什麼會叫做loo，有好幾種說法，有些是說從法文regardez l'eau 的諧音 gardyloo 來的。飛機上的廁所我們說 "lavatory ['læ•və•tɔ•rɪ]"，在軍中則為 "latrine [lə'trɪn]"。至於 WC "Water Closet" 很少聽到。

珍在廁所。

Jane's in the loo.

—— 《Coupling 1x04 Inferno》

✅ 上廁所 "take a bio-break"

"use the restroom / use the ladies'." 這兩句就很好用了。其他還有很多說法，倒不一定要都會說，但是這種非常基本的東西，多聽得懂幾句也不錯，生理方面的需求 "answer the call of nature / Take a bio-break / pee break." 或用到剛才那個loo。 例如 "I have to go to the loo / I'm off to the loo." 還有這個我得去上大號／小號 "I have to take a dump / piss."

我尿的很快馬上回來。

I'm gonna take a quick pee break.

—— 《2 Broke Girls 02x14》

✅ I need to go somewhere.

聽到這句你要是問他Where？這個就好笑了，如果感覺他是在問你，指給他化妝室在哪裡就行，或者他自己會去找，只是跟你告知一聲，那你也可以回一句：

去吧去吧，該去就去，快去快去。

例如 If you gotta go, you gotta go./ When you got to go, you got to go.

2.2 日本精選 阿美橫町歡樂購、夢幻壽司啖好食

💬 情境對話

MP3 008

Swenson
剛才晚餐吃的不多，我現在好餓。
I did not have much dinner. Now I'm starving.

Swenson
逛完アメ（阿美橫町）。累死了。
After shopping in the A-Mei district, I'm spent.

麥可
逛一天的街很累？在阿富汗的時候你怎麼不説累？
A long day? Why didn't you say anything in Afghanistan?

麥可
那你想吃什麼？
What are you thinking about?

Swenson
我突然好想吃壽司。
I just have a craving for sushi.

麥可
去哪家壽司餐廳，迴轉壽司？還是蓋高尚的壽司餐廳？
Which sushi restaurant do you wanna go to? A conveyor belt sushi joint or a really nice sushi restaurant?

Swenson
一般我都是吃迴轉壽司。
I always go for conveyor [kən'vεɚ] belt sushi.

Swenson
既然都到了日本，所以夢幻壽司料理才是王道。
And now here we are in Japan, where a king sushi fantasy can come true.

在日本吃壽司有什麼特別的餐桌禮儀嗎？
Do you know about sushi etiquette in Japan?

我聽說吃壽司要用手，而不是用筷子，喜金A嗎？
I heard that you should have sushi with your hands, not chopsticks. Is that true?

這個嘛⋯有些上流美是這麼說的，但是，當然你可以用筷子。
Well… I've heard some ladies who lunch say that, but, ofc you can use chopsticks.

一個有用的小提示。
Here is a slightly helpful tip.

用魚肉那面沾醬油，而不是米飯的那面。
Dip the fish-side into the soy sauce, not the rice-side.

如果你用米飯那面沾醬油，飯糰可能會散開。
If you dip the rice-side, the rice might fall apart.

把壽司上下顛倒然後沾醬油⋯用筷子好像有點難。
Flip nigiri upside down and dip only the fish-side into the soy sauce… it's kind of difficult with chopsticks.

嗯啊，如果用手比較輕鬆的話你就用手。
Yeah, use your hands, if it's easier for you.

還有這點你可以參考一下。
And one more piece of advice.

有些貴婦喜歡把甜薑直接沾了醬油後，再去沾壽司上面的肉。
Some trophy wives dip gari directly into the soy sauce then tip the sushi with it.

麥可

這樣看起來貌似很優雅，但是有的壽司師傅不喜歡客人這樣。
It looks very elegant, but some sushi chefs don't appreciate it.

麥可

甜薑的味道很重，會蓋過肉的味道而嚐不出來新鮮魚肉的原味。
Gari tastes strong, so it could spoil the original flavor of the fresh fish.

Swenson

那甜薑什麼時候吃呢？
So when will we have gari ['gɑrɪ]?

麥可

在不同口味的壽司之間作為一個味蕾清新劑，清除口腔中上一道食物的餘味。
In between different pieces of sushi as a palette cleanser [k'lɛnzɚ], refreshing your taste buds for another bite.

麥可

也有增進食欲的作用。
And it helps work up an appetite.

麥可

我看就這家。這地方看起來還不錯，你覺得呢？
I think this is the one. This place looks good, don't you think?

Swenson

哇，這家壽司店氣氛真好。
Wow, this sushi restaurant has a good vibe.

Swenson

嗯…從哪個開始吃好呢？
Mmm... what should I have first?

麥可

一般來説先選味道比較淡的魚開始吃，比如鯛魚或比目魚壽司。
Generally, it's said that you start by eating fish with a lighter flavor, such as sea bream (たい) or flounder (ひらめ).

然後呢，吃點味道較重的好比鮪魚跟海膽壽司。
And then, move on to fish with a heavier flavor, such as tuna (マグロ) or sea urchin (ウニ).

妥當也。
Okie DoKie.

這這這，這個菜單上面沒有標價。
Ooops, this menu doesn't have prices listed.

是的，這裡的壽司是時價。所以，這壽司餐廳在點菜單上…
Yep, the sushi here has its spot price. So, the sushi restaurants' menu…

…不會標出價錢。
…might not show the prices.

你為什麼一直在流汗？
Why are you sweating?

沒有為什麼…
Just because…

你應該有帶信用卡吧，對吧？
You did bring your credit card, didn't you?

☆ 單詞與句型

✓ 才是王道／才對 "FTW"

for the win。必勝，才是王道。這個在口語中不用另外加動詞就這樣用，書面打字的時候，通常是縮寫成FTW，而不必全部拼出來。

這樣才對！

That's what makes it right!

—— 《*Everybody Loves Raymond 05x08 Young Girl*》

（Scene：謝耳朵未經Leonard的同意，把他Facebook的狀態改為戀愛中，導致Leonard大抓狂。）

LEONARD：別！我不想再聽你說一個字。

Don't even! I don't want to hear another word out of you.

（Scene：然後發現Stephanie也將她的狀態改為跟Leonard戀愛中，這時謝耳朵可得意了。）

SHELDON：如果能允許我再次說話，聽謝耳朵博士的才是王道。
If I am permitted to speak again, Dr. Sheldon Cooper ftw.

—— 《*The Big Bang 02x09*》

✔ 要表達什麼什麼才是王道，還有 "…is the way to go"，
"…is the answer"。

如果你想要玩真的，你最好準備充分。活誘餌才是王道。
If you're after serious game, you'd better come ready. Live bait is the way to go.

—— 《*Banshee 01x02*》

我要用咒語打敗你。不，科學才是王道。
I'll strike you down with my spell! No, science is the answer!

—— 《*Cougar Town 2x17*》

✅ FTL

必敗，弱爆了 "For the loss"。

筷子兄弟必敗！龐麥郎君我要給你生孩子！
The Chopsticks Brothers FTL! Punmanlon my love I want to have your baby!

—— 《My Dc Shoes Humping Humping》

✅ 當然 "Ofc"

"Of course" 口語英文裡的縮寫很多，有些冷門的無可無不可了，大家可以自行上網搜尋。這裡是幾句常見常用的：

- Afk：away from keyboard，人不在。
- brb rbfrom keyboar，離開一下。
- Ttyl tylrom keyboard，無可無等下聊。
- Nvm vmlrom keyb，沒事。
- imho mhorom keyboard，無可無不可了依臣愚見。
- imho in my honest opinion，肺腑之言。
- tyt yt見rom keyboard，慢慢來。

✅ 甜薑 "gari"

ガリ，sushi ginger，pickled ginger，日本甜薑。

✅ 氣氛真好 "Has good vibes."

vibe是vibration的縮寫，使用的也相當普遍，可以用在中文的氣氛，氛圍，局面，感應感覺到。"A vibe, vibes, ambience, atmosphere, mood" 都可以用來表達氣氛。

再說，我喜歡那裡，那裡氣氛很棒。

Besides, I like it in there, has a good vibe.

—《Person Of Interest 01x12》

我喜歡那的氣氛。

I like the ambience.

—《Prison Break 1x01》

離這裡不遠有個地方充滿了適宜人居的氣息。

Not so far from here there's a very lively atmosphere.

—《Boardwalk Empire 1x04》

這並非我所想的氣氛。

Well, this isn't exactly the mood that I wanted to set.

—《Be With You 01x01》

把衝突的雷管拔掉 "defuses conflict" 那衝突就不會一發不可收拾了，所以 "defuses conflict" 指緩和氣氛。很多不必要的衝突，導火線往往來自於不恰當的言語，傷人的話其實不亞於扔塊石頭到人家臉上，除了顯得自己沒 "etiquette" 外，舌頭常常也會引來拳頭。

我發現在恰當的時候插話總能緩和緊張的氣氛。

I find that interjecting at precisely the right moment often defuses conflict.

—《Pushing Daisies 02x07》

你剛剛是怎麼了？你不喜歡查莉嗎？她還好啦，我不知道，我只是感覺跟她相處的氛圍不是很好。

Do you not like Charlie? She's okay. I don't know. I just don't get a really good vibe from her.

—— 《*Friends 09x22 The Donor*》

✅ 流汗 "**sweating**"

臉不紅氣不喘，不費吹灰之力，可以用"Without even breaking a sweat"，老外形容冷汗的方式很有趣 ^^，我們來瞅瞅以下的例句，各種sweat的用法：

你現在滿身大汗。

You are really sweaty.

—— 《*Mixology S1x02 Liv And Ron*》

拿兩個建築工人來說，有個很壯的他能在一小時內臉不紅氣不喘的砌4面牆。

Take two construction workers. One is strong and can raise four walls in an hour without even breaking a sweat.

—— 《*Justice 08 What's A Fair Start*？／*what Do We Deserve*》

為什麼呢？親愛的？為了沒有邀請我，還是你說謊騙我呢？

For what, dear? For not inviting me, or for lying about it?

喔，天！我出了一身冷汗。

Oh, my God! My ass is sweating.

—— 《*Friends 08x20 The Baby Shower*》

我很緊張，我的胃在翻騰，我都出冷汗了。

I'm nervous, my stomach's bubbling, I get sweaty armpits.

—— 《Cat Run》

不用sweat，用nosebleed

下面這句很寫實，我捨不得刪 ^^

你剛才說「有位懷孕的女士要見你」，嚇出我一身冷汗。

You just said "Pregnant woman here to see you," give me a fucking nosebleed.

—— 《Boardwalk Empire 1x01 Boardwalk Empire》

✔ 沒有為什麼／不為什麼 "just because"

類似之前有流行過一句無厘頭的回答，因為豆漿濃，這種語感，有些話人家問了你不想回答或不知道怎麼回答，隨便搪塞一句。

沒啥為什麼，就告訴你們這些人老子不幹。

Not for nothin', but I'm not doin' it, y'all.

—— 《Cougar Town 2x06》

那你為什麼還要問？沒有為什麼，只是覺得有點幼稚。

Why do you ask? No reason, it just seems a bit naive.

—— 《Hitman》

人們彼此照應沒有什麼為什麼，只因為這是正確該做的事。

People taking care of each other for no other reason than it was the right thing to do.

—— 《World Trade Center》

✅ 禮儀 "etiquette ['ɛ•tɪ•kɪt]"

這個字可以是禮儀，禮節，家教，教養。網路禮節 "netiquette" 一起記，
是network（網路）與etiquette（禮節）的結合。

多教我些禮節。

Teach me more about etiquette.

—— 《Miss March 2009》

我的社交技巧很好，還有…語言，禮節教養，高爾夫，懂滑雪。

I've got great communication skills, and...Languages, etiquette, golf...
Knowing how to ski.

—— 《Secret Diary Of A Call Girl 01x08》

👍 達人提點

✅ 日本整個氛圍就是很重禮節

想到日本就會想到風景漂亮乾淨，注重禮節。其實也有部分日本人覺得
各種繁文縟節實在太多了，但是整個社會的大環境社會風氣 "climate" 就
是這樣。

可現在外面的大環境這是這樣。

But there's a climate out there right now.

—— 《The Practice 01x04》

在當下這種局面，就算你再怎麼試也沒辦法把文章寫得更狂野了。

You couldn't write a paper that clashes more violently with the
current climate if you were trying.

—— 《In The Loop 2009》

✅ 如果有抽菸的團員

記得要提醒有抽菸的團員帶一種隨身的煙灰袋。定點如十字路口，天橋上的公設煙灰箱跟7-eleven門口可以抽，或者上面有貼標籤註明可以抽菸的餐廳或咖啡館，有些有時段限制，同一家餐廳有的時段可以抽菸，有的時段不行，要注意看一下標籤。某些地方會有穿著類似警察制服的工作人員，會勸導你不要邊走邊抽菸，是屬於一種區域管理規則。沒有警察的地方也盡量不要邊走邊抽，給人的感覺不好。

2.3 線上旅展・兩萬有找 FUN遊淺草寺、有病治病無病強身

情境對話

MP3 009

ピコちゃん
哇，你看門口掛的那個無敵大燈籠！
Wow, look at that super huge lantern hanging at the gate!

麥可
那是雷門的提燈，是淺草寺最具代表性的標誌之一。
That's the lantern of Thunder Gate. One of the Asakusa Shrine's most representative symbols.

ピコちゃん
真的好大一個喔，還有那些黑衣人是誰…
That's really huge, and who are those guys in black...

ピコちゃん
啊，我知道了，他們是人力車伕。
Ah, I got it. They are rickshaw runners.

麥可
對啊，你可以坐那個逛一圈。
Yep, you can go for a ride around the block.

ピコちゃん
我想坐，免費的嗎？
I'd like to go for a ride, is it free?

麥可
人家靠這個賺錢的。我們先去淺草寺吧。
They are going to charge for this service. Let's go to Sensoji first.

等一下！我看到一個很特別的房子！？
Wait! Do you see that special building?

在哪裡？
Where?

那棟看起來就像一杯蓋滿泡沫的巨無霸啤酒的建築物。
That building which looks like a frothy billion-ounce glass beer.

那是朝日啤酒的總部。
That's Asahi's headquarter.

旁邊那個是晴空塔（天空樹）。這裡有很多賣紀念品的店而且觀光客人潮很多。
Next to it is Tokyo Skytree. There are a lot of souvenir shops at Nakamise-dori and lots of tourists.

在仲見世商店街的最裡面，你會看到淺草寺，我們等一下在那裏集合。
At the end of Nakamise-dori street, you'll see Senso-ji Temple. Later, we round up there.

嗨！領隊～
Hi! Michael~

嗨。畢可強。
Hi. ピコちゃん.

你看這個，我找到這些好漂亮的筷子。日本的東西真的好可愛捏。
Check this, I found those beautiful chopsticks. Japanese stuff is really cute.

ピコちゃん 對了，剛才我看到有些人，圍著一個冒煙的大香爐。
BTW, I saw some people gathering around a big smoking censer.

麥可 他們在薰香裡淨身，有病治病無病強身你懂的。
They are bathing in cense smoke. It is believed that fanning the smoke onto them will heal diseases or help them grow stronger.

麥可 還有人會就著香爐的煙在頭上揉一揉。
Some of them rub their heads with smoke.

ピコちゃん 我來拍幾張照片好了。
Let me take some pictures.

麥可 去吧…等等！
Go ahead... Wait!

麥可 有一個好地方可以拍照，你看到那個很大的銀杏樹嗎？
There is a good place for taking photos. Do you see that big ginkgo tree?

麥可 在樹旁邊，你會看到在地上有一個眺望點。
By the tree, you will see a photo op site on the ground.

麥可 站那裡拍的淺草寺最漂亮。
That's the best place to take a photo of Senso-ji Temple.

ピコちゃん 這麼美的畫面…嘖嘖，假文青該説點什麼吧。
What a scene... heh, heh, you can't deny it.

ピコちゃん 前排。
Front row.

麥可 別捉急，醖釀ing。
No rush, it's fermenting.

夕陽的點點餘暉穿過樹影，灑在如畫般的淺草寺…我嗯…換你了。
Picturesque Senso-ji baskin' in the sunset behind trees... I umm... Your turn.

我不知道怎麼接…
I don't know the next verse...

那這篇就到這裡了。
The end.

逛一圈 "around the block"

逛一圈，繞一圈，其他中文裡會講什麼一圈的。

於是我跑去周圍逛了一圈，假裝我是個海盜。
So I ran around, pretending to be a pirate.

—— 《*Boardwalk Empire 1x05 Nights In Ballygran*》

多逛逛，比如去百貨公司買襪子，不直接坐電梯上五樓買了就回家，多逛了一圈。

這裡？繞一圈嘛。走。
In here? A detour. Go.

—— 《*The Lovely Bones 2009*》

停車或溜冰，再轉一圈，再繞一圈，再兜一圈

大家都有這樣的經驗，再繞一圈找停車位，或溜冰還想再玩多溜一圈

"One more time around." 好了，就停在這裡 "Okay, just pull over right there."

再來一圈。去吧，再一圈，再一圈。

One more time around. Go on. One more time. One more time.

—— 《*True Detective 01x05*》

➔ 賽車的一圈

我的車領先你一圈，哥們　你落後一圈，小夥伴。

I'm a lap ahead of you, brah. You're a lap behind, dude.

—— 《*The Listener 03x02*》

➔ 人，身體轉一圈。

轉一圈，小美人。讓我們看看你的小屁股。

Spin around, cupcake. Let's see the caboose!

—— 《*Modern Family 01x18*》

神經錢德把我轉一圈…

Crazy Chandler spun me...

—— 《*Friends 03x03 The Jam*》

➔ 其他

膠帶再纏一圈吧，緊一點，再緊一點。

Maybe one more layer. And tight, really tight.

—— 《*Modern Family 01x24*》

鬼門關走一圈回來已經夠倒楣了。

It's bad enough we went to hell and back.

—— 《Homeland 02x07》

✅一杯蓋滿泡沫的 "a frothy glass"

a frothy glass of beer，一杯蓋著泡沫的啤酒，啤酒泡沫是beer foam，相對於a glass of beer with the bubble foam at the top，a frothy glass of beer更簡單好記又地道喔。

✅旁邊 "next to / by the"

表達旁邊，可以用next to、by、near，站在旁邊，Stand over，比較遠的旁邊，on the other side。

→ 如果用next to

你得坐在帥哥旁邊。

You'll be sitting next to Hot Guy.

—— 《Friends 08x22 Where Rachel Is Late》

→ 用by

如果是浴室旁邊的櫃子呢？

How about the closet by the bathroom?

—— 《Friends 08x14 The Secret Closet》

→ 用 **near**

聽著，羅斯在你旁邊嗎？

Listen, is... is Ross near you?

—— 《Friends 09x09 Rachel's Phone Number》

→ **Stand over**

站旁邊看著爐子，翻烤著煎餅。

Standing over the stove, flipping pancakes.

—— 《Fringe 01x20》

→ **the other side**，旁邊，另一邊。

別撞到一邊的垃圾桶。

Not hit the dumpster on the other side.

—— 《Friends 07x12 Where They're Up All Night》

✔ 集合 "**round up**"

集合的英文怎麼說？"round up / gather up / gather around / gather together / assemble" 集合本團所有的旅客 "Round up all the tourists in this tour group." 下午集合後吃自助午餐 "Buffet lunch followed by afternoon meeting."

我們齊聚於此來見證這個偉大的時刻。

As we gather together for this great occasion.

—— 《24Hrs 08x24》

這次集會的意義何在？

So what's the point of this gathering?

—— 《*Boardwalk Empire 1x11*》

在上帝的註視之下，我們今天在此齊聚一堂。

We are gathered here today in the sight of God.

—— 《*Everybody Loves Raymond 07x24 Robert's Wedding*》

女生的天性就是和其他女生聚在一起…然後吱吱喳喳。

It is always the nature of the female to gather with other females... And screech.

—— 《*Everybody Loves Raymond 08x20 Blabbermouths*》

來賓們，請收拾好東西，到前門來。好了，女士們，結束了。

Patrons, gather up your stuff, start heading to the front door. All right, ladies, let's wrap this up.

—— 《*Banshee 02x07*》

✔ 全體集合 "all assemble"

在學校大廳全體集合 "All assemble in the school hall."
集合點 "meeting point / assembly point / gathering point"

她們現在都坐在「馬可美國全美披薩店」，現在那成了恨我的人集合點了。

They're both sitting together at what is now, "Marco's All-American Pizzeria, U. S. A.", and now it's a gathering place for everyone who hates me.

—— 《*Everybody Loves Raymond 05x21 Lets Fix Robert*》

✅ 假文青 "hipster scum"

時尚時尚最時尚，十萬青年十萬軍，東山飄雨西山晴，三教九流皆文青。聞腋青年最近可謂是萬人黑不夠，表示討厭的歌有這首《Pillow Case Kisser By Skinned Teen》Pillow Case Kisser指找不到人玩親親，只能夜夜獨自對著枕頭的人：

你們這些裝什麼裝的小青年。

To the kids in the classroom.

你們就等著被摸頭吧。

Can't you wait until... When they gang up and get at you.

想裝屌卻裝不出來。

You wanna be so cool but you know you'll never make it.

想玩內涵又被人一眼看穿。

You think you've got soul but I know you have to fake it.

―― 《Skins 03x03 Pillow Case Kisser By Skinned Teen》

不排斥hipster的可以搜下這首洗腦神曲《Yacht Summer Song》，從1分15秒開始聽，我覺得還蠻好聽的，歌詞很簡單只有四句：

Summer came up and sang a song♪♪

When summer came up we sang along♪.

We stayed up talking all night long♪.

So move your feet to the summer song♪♪.

―― 《Yacht Summer Song》

君要臣脫，臣不得不脫。不是那種脫衣舞酒吧啦，我是說假掰文青的冷知識酒吧。

If I have to strip, I have to strip. Not that kind of bar, the hipster trivia bar.

—— 《*2 Broke Girls 02x17*》

達人提點

✅ 美制單位

英文裡的單位不是常用的人會不太習慣。下面有些必懂的縮寫，付上常見的價錢及單位，大家用點想像力，或上網逛逛美國超市，輪廓會比較清楚，比較有概念。比如搜尋shoprite進去後點一下右上方那個很大的傳單，畫面變了以後按categories，選meat & seafood就會跑出一堆東西了。

➡ 每份八盎司 **"8 oz / per serving"**

oz，ounce的縮寫是oz不是oc。21盎司大概一斤，600g。一塊6盎司牛排的大小，感覺像漢堡裡夾的那塊肉然後從旁邊凸出來，一般牛排館你看到的大小約為8～10盎司一人份，16盎司就很大塊了，也有些標榜大塊肉的牛排屋是20盎司起跳的，這樣有沒有飢餓感（誤）畫面感？^^

➡ 丁骨牛排一磅十三塊九毛九 **"T-bone steak $13. 99 / Lb"**

Lb "libra pondo / per pound"，with coupon有時可以買到10元以下的價錢，是LB不是1B。450g剛好是在半斤300g跟一斤600g之間的一半。

→ 牛奶一加侖四塊半 "milk $4. 5 / gal (gallon) "
一加侖等於128盎司等於3. 785 liter."

→ 鳳梨每個三塊九毛九 "pineapple $3. 99 / ea (each) "

→ 草莓一盒五塊九九 "strawberry $5. 99 / 3bxs (box / boxes) "

→ 中小型蛤俐十二塊九毛九36入一袋 "$12. 99 / 36-ct (count) Bag Live middle-neck clams"

→ 六個1包 "6 pcs (pieces) / PK (package) "

→ 梨子十六塊九毛九一箱 "pear $16. 99 / cs (case) "

一些民生必需品是永遠不應該漲價的。我現在腦海中想到的就有衛生棉條和超大瓶啤酒。

That people need in an emergency that you never raise the price on. Off the top of my head, tampons and 40-ounce beers.

—— 《2 Broke Girls 1x13 And The Secret Ingredient》

2.4 戀戀韓風·高雄出發 首爾機場、文明人請排隊

💬 情境對話

MP3 010

小螃蟹機長
女士們、先生們。
Ladies and Gentlemen.

小螃蟹機長
我們深表歉意因為機場氣候問題，耽誤您寶貴的時間。
We apologize for the delay due to bad weather conditions over the airport.

小螃蟹機長
現在飛機已達定位並完全停穩。
Our plane has pulled into the gate and has stopped completely.

小螃蟹機長
下機時，請您檢查一下是否已帶齊了所有的隨身行李。
Please ensure that you have all your belongings when you disembark [dɪsəm'bɑrk].

小螃蟹機長
感謝您今天搭乘新加坡航空公司的班機。
Thank you for choosing Singapore Airlines for your travel today.

小螃蟹機長
期待再相會。
We look forward to serving you again.

麥可
麻煩都到這邊來好嗎？注意聽一下，各位。
Would you all gather over here? Attention, everybody.

有人要上廁所嗎？沒有？很好。
Anyone need to use the restroom? No? Great.

航班有點誤點，來我們走電動步道。
The flight was a bit late. We take the moving sidewalk.

好，到了護照檢查區。我們就在這裡把隊伍排起來。
Okay, here is the Immigration Inspection Area. Let's line up in here.

請大家準備好護照，出入境單，跟海關單。
Please have your passport, E / D card and Customs Declaration in your hand.

這樣大概要排隊等多久？
How long do we have to wait in this line?

這通關隊伍看起來要等半個小時。
It looks like a half-hour long immigration queue I'd say.

是喔？
Really?

稍安勿躁。我打個電話跟導遊說一下。
Relax. Let me inform the tour guide.

那女人插隊！
That young woman cut in front of us!

那邊有人在大吼大叫。
There're some people raising their voice over there.

嘿！不可以插隊，回去。
Hey, no cutting! Go back there.

111

Jane Blow

妳不可以插隊！排回去！
You can't cut in line! Back of the line.

Maverick

又來一個男的插到我們隊伍的前面了。
Another guy cut in front of us.

Jane Blow

大家聽著，我們這裡有個插隊的！
Guys! We got a line cutter here!

Line cutters

裝傻ing。
Act dumb.

Jane Blow

你們大家有沒有看到他們這些人皮有多厚？
Have you guys seen how brazen they are?

Jane Blow

不要臉！
Cheeky!

Maverick

看起來這些插隊的都是同一團的。
Seems those Lline cutters are from the same tourist group.

Maverick

這些奇葩是從哪裡來的？（傻眼）
Who are those wackos? *go round-eyed*

麥可

他們開了另一條護照檢查櫃台，走我們過去，走！
They've opened up another passport control counter. Let's move, go!

Maverick

我拍了幾張這些沒素質的人。
I took some pictures of those people who have no decency.

Maverick

我要貼到臉書上。
I want to post them on facebook..

機場不能拍照或錄影，你拍的的照片可能會被沒收喔（**比較** topography [tə'pɑ•grə•fɪ] 地形學）。
No photography [fə'tɑ•grə•fɪ] or filming at the airport, or you may have your pictures confiscated.

沒被抓到就不算，下次多小心點囉。
Unless you get caught, be more careful next time.

我們去行李轉盤，導遊等很久了。
Let's move to Baggage Carousel. The guide's been waiting.

☆ 單詞與句型

✓ 航空公司 "airlines"

旅遊的時候，會遇到各式各樣的服務員有很多種，各種各有不同的習慣說法。空勤空姐空少 "flight attendant / cabin crew" 機長 "Captain"，副機師是FO "First Officer"。聽膩了規規矩矩的機艙廣播嗎？來個Hilarious funny Flight Attendant Announcement，搜尋以上幾個關鍵字就可以找到一堆搞笑的，下是一個例子還有很多 ^^

各位先生女士早，歡迎您搭乘長榮航空波音787，我們飛得比巴士快很多。
Good Morning, Ladies and Gentlemen, welcome you aboard Eva Air Boeing 787, we're much faster than the bus.

跟我們其中的一人結婚，您就有免費機票。機長和全體機組人員祝您旅途愉快。

Marry one of us and you'll fly free. The captain and crew we invite you to sit back, and enjoy the flight.

當您離開飛機的時候，請記得帶上所有的隨身行李。

As you exit the plane, make sure to gather all of your belongings.

任何留下的東西都會被空姐平均分贓，請不要留下小孩或配偶。

Anything left behind will be distributed evenly among the flight attendants, please do not leave children or spouses.

✅ 護照檢查櫃台 "passport control counter"

入境時，到了護照檢查區，這時要拿掉護照套打開護照，並準備好入出境卡跟海關單，排隊時注意不同通道指示團員排在正確的通關隊伍，例如 "group / fit"，"foreigner / local citizen"，海關櫃檯輪到你時，海關官員會給你蓋個入境章，如果delay，手機要開啟漫遊打電話或短信通知Local，順便告知從哪個Gate出去以免Local枯候。

海關櫃檯 "Passport Control Counter"。也可以說border control counter，或at the Immigration Counter，最懶的說法就說個checkpoint。‹cf.› the immigration checkpoint是邊哨檢查站。

- Please have your passport or identity card ready for inspection.
  準備好入出境卡跟海關單。
- immigration queue，通關隊伍。
- Immigration officer，海關官員。

・Entry stamp，入境章；Exit stamp，是出境章；Passport stamp，統稱為護照章。

把隊伍排起來 "line it up"

排隊時如果人多，提醒團員盡量緊靠不要讓某幾個團員落單到後面，眼觀八方如有開新櫃，指揮團員過去，如果有人數限制，只過去了部分團員，試試與機場人員溝通，告知我們是同一個旅遊團的 "Group Package Tour" 就這幾個看能不能讓他們一起過去。排隊等 "wait in line." 排這條隊 "stand in this line."

是李斯特雷德，他們一會兒就過來了，排一長串等著給你上拷呢。
It's Lestrade. Says they're all coming over here right now. Queuing up to slap on the handcuffs.
—— 《Sherlock 02x03 The Reichenbach Fall》

最好早點去，你知道排隊的人很多。
You better get up there early 'cause you know how those lines are.
—— 《Everybody Hates Chris 02X15》

喂，不准插隊！
Hey, no cutting!

冷靜。虛驚一場，他只是換位置了。
Calm down. False alarm, he's just doing fair tradesies.

說真的，別小題大作了。
Honestly, stop overreacting to cutting.

我去最後排隊，這位置給保羅。

I'm going to the back of the line. This spot's for Paul.

—《New Girl 01x06》

✅ 皮有多厚 "brazen" ；不要臉 "cheeky ['tʃi•kɪ]"

明目張膽，厚顏無恥的。 近音字 美女 "chicky ['tʃɪ•kɪ]"。

你對上帝的褻瀆是更加的明目張膽了。

A little more brazen in your blasphemy ['blæs•fə•mɪ].

—《Everybody Loves Raymond 04x14 Prodigal Son》

無恥啊，真是太無恥了。

That's low. That's really low.

—《Hawaii Five O 01x20》

我以為你不會這麼無恥我知道。有時候我挺有品的。

I thought you were better than that. I know. I am sometimes.

—《New Girl 01x05》

唐璜（西班牙楚留香）身邊總不缺漂亮的妞兒。

Don Juan got a little chicky on the side.

—《Person Of Interest 01x09》

✅ 不要臉然後呢，就會demean，貶低，使…蒙羞

她接下來所做的，讓新郎蒙羞，讓她自己蒙羞，讓整個人類為之蒙羞。

Then she proceeds to do things that demean the groom, herself and really, the entire human race.

—《How I Met Your Mother 02x19 Bachelor Party Repack》

一個人為什麼願意一直幹這種低賤的工作…

Why would a person stay in such a demeaning job...

　　　　　—— 《Friends 03x11 Chandler Cant Remember Which Sister》

費爾德先生這個荒謬的測試，是片面主觀武斷的，而且侮辱人的。

This ridiculous test of Mr. Infeld's, it's arbitrary and demeaning.

　　　　　　　　　　　　—— 《Franklin And Bash 02x05》

✅ 沒素質 "no decency"

或者用indecency。沒教養，沒家教，沒禮貌，沒水準，不得體，有失莊重。Don't you have any shame, any sense of decency？你難道沒有一點嗎羞恥心嗎？沒有一點教養？基本的禮貌，起碼的禮貌，common decency。A basic sense of decency。

你要不要臉？

Have you no decency?

　　　　　　　　　　　　　　—— 《24Hrs 08x09》

她沒有意識到自己三八過頭了。喔，你認為這樣是不得體？

Who doesn't realize that she's crossed the line of decency. Oh, you think this is indecent?

　　　　　　　　　　—— 《Everybody Loves Raymond 09x04》

你才是那個以自我為中心的人，連禮貌性的意思意思吃兩口都不肯。

You're the one who's self centered, don't even have the decency to eat it.

　　　　　　　　—— 《Everybody Loves Raymond 03x08 The Article》

有什麼規定說我們不能在下午四點就開始吸古柯鹼嗎？

Is there any rule that says we can't just start doing the coke right now circa 4:00 p.m.?

我是想表達，規矩倒沒有，但人格上不允許。

I mean, no rule but human decency.

—— 《Girls 02x03》

✔ 裝傻 "act dumb"

裝傻，例如 play dumb。

你裝傻裝的不像，瑞秋。

You're too smart to play dumb, Rachel.

—— 《House Of Cards 01x13》

別跟我裝傻，彼得。

Don't play dumb with me Peter.

—— 《House Of Cards 01x01》

✔ 裝可愛，賣萌

naif是法語的naïf 例如 naive，天真的，涉世未深的。法語faux-naïf 例如 faux-naif [fo ˌnaɪˈif]，faux的x不發音，人工的或矯揉做作的天真 "artificially or affectedly naive"，裝傻裝天真。裝可愛也可以用act adorable或act cute。 例如 "I don't believe she never heard about condom, kind of faux-naif."

別再裝可愛，行唄，讓我們實際點。

And stop being all cutesy and whatever, fine. Let's get real.

—— 《New Girl 01x15》

你是以為我認不出自己的字，或你就是想裝可愛？

Did you think I wouldn't recognize my own words, or are you just trying to be cute?

—— 《Perception 01x08》

他在裝傻，因為他知道我們喜歡呆呆萌萌 。

He's being silly because he knows we enjoy the silliness.

—— 《Friends 06x03 Rosss Denial》

那我們就不裝可愛了。

Let's not pretend to be naive.

—— 《House Of Cards 02x06》

達人提點

✔ 出境

到了機場，過了Information Counter機場服務櫃台後，首先在Airport Office航空公司的機場辦事處，把護照交給送機，問送機Check-in Counter在那裡（報到櫃台，掛行李那個櫃台），然後指引Passengers旅客在報到櫃台排行李，注意Departure Boards出境航班告示版，看Gate登機口在那裡，並於機場說明會告知旅客。候機時，注意看出境航班告示版，登機門有時會變，有些機場很大，不同登機門之間距離很遠，趕過去也要時間。

→ 關於人有三急

- 上飛機前提醒旅客在出發機場或飛機上，能上廁所的就先上，這樣等一下通關會比較不用久等。

- 過空橋下機後，先就近在第一個洗手間外面集合旅客，問有沒有人要上化妝室的，如果有就走一般步道（非電動步道）到第二個廁所，通常人會比較少一點。
- 到了行李轉盤後，上車前再問一次，這要看旅館，餐館，或第一個景點離機場多遠，有的要拉一個多小時的車。

✔ 行李轉盤 "Baggage Carousel"

Carousel [ˌkæ•rəˈsɛl]，看到站航班資訊看板 "Arrival Board"，找到自己的航班後，上面會寫此航班的行李在幾號行李轉盤 "baggage / luggage Carousel"，有的機場空橋會有告示，有些沒有，看到後就告知客人我們在幾號行李轉盤集合，取行李時只取自己的行李，如果不是自己的行李，就算是陌生人請幫忙，甚至是海關人員問是不是你的要你去拿，都不要去碰。

2.5 韓國現折1,000 東大門快樂購、下雪了怎能 沒有炸雞配啤酒

💬 **情境對話**

MP3 011

麥可
嗶波！又到了瘋狂大血拼的時候了。
Yipee! Time for a shopping spree.

麥可
批發價，絕對是你的菜。
Wholesale prices, you gotta love it.

麥可
下午自由活動好好玩吧。
Enjoy your free afternoon.

麥可
等一下我們5點半就在這裡集合，首爾時間。（**比較** Soul是靈魂）
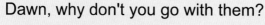
We'll meet up at five thirty right here, Seoul Time.

麥可
晨曦，你怎麼不跟著他們走？
Dawn, why don't you go with them?

Dawn
我為什麼不願意走？
You don't think I will?

Dawn
雙腳攏麻去，是要安怎走？
I can't feel my legs, how do I walk?

麥可
你要先找地方坐下。來瓶可樂？
You might want to take a seat. Coke?

不好了。我腳痛死了。
Uh-oh. My feet are killing me.

我還真需要來點這可樂／可卡因。
I do kinda need this coke.

有好點嗎？
Any better?

比較像是隱隱作痛的感覺。
It's more of a dull ache.

然後刺刺的好像有螞蟻在咬。
And it's tingly.

我沒法穿這種木底鞋走路。
I can't walk in clogs.

也許是襪子太緊了腳踝麻了。
Maybe the socks made your ankles numb.

也許根本不是襪子的原因。
Maybe it wasn't the socks after all.

死馬當活馬醫試試看。
Anyway, give it a try.

你說對了！現在我感覺好多了。
You are right! Now I feel way better.

但我在意自己的腳趾腫腫的，不好看。
But I am concerned about my swollen toes. They don't look good.

可能這幾天路走多了，等會冰敷一下。
Could be from all the walking these past few days. Put some ice on it later.

你要貼點痠痛藥布嗎？
You want some pain relief patches?

你現在有嗎？
You have some here?

沒有。
Nope.

痠痛藥布我留在旅館房間，等下會給你。
I left the patches in the hotel room. You can get them later.

等我們回旅館後。
After we head back to the hotel.

腳抬高，冰敷個20分鐘。
Lift your legs up. Just ice them for 20 minutes.

這樣可以消腫。
It can reduce swelling.

你平常也可試著做點簡單省事的例行運動來鍛鍊腳部肌肉。
You might wanna try a quick and easy workout routine to strengthen your legs muscles.

快看！那邊有個人在跳麥可傑克遜的舞耶。
Look! There's a guy dancing like Michael Jackson over there.

模仿得不錯，不是嗎？
Not bad, huh?

要拍照趕快。警察很快就會把他攆出去了。
Take some pics, hurry up. The police will give him the bum's rush soon.

麥可

（回到旅館後 "Back at the hotel"）你的撒隆巴斯來了。
Here comes your Salonpas.

麥可

哇，這個謝謝你喔。
Wow, thank you for this.

Dawn

嘿，你要來吃炸雞跟韓國啤酒嗎？
Hey, you want to stay for fried chicken and Cass?

Dawn

哦，沒什麼，我不打擾了，就是把這個拿給你。好夢。
Oh, it's all right. I won't trouble you, but I brought you this. Sweet dreams!

麥可

你也是。
You too.

Dawn

☆ 單詞與句型

✓ 瘋狂大血拼 "shopping spree [spri]"

歡樂大血拼，瘋狂大購物，spree這個字有「嬉戲打鬧」的意思，也可解釋成瘋狂沉迷與歡樂。她今天又去血拼了。Today she went on a shopping spree again。

所以我們的話題不是在「買好康購物網」血拼大採購。
So we're not talking about a shopping spree at Best Buy.

—— 《*Person Of Interest 01x18*》

她和她同夥正在瘋狂連續搶銀行。

Her and her partner went on a bank robbing spree.

—— 《Hawaii Five O 02x23》

我很想在一個發生過瘋狂連環槍擊案的地方開店。

Obviously I wanna start a business in a place where there was a shooting spree.

—— 《2 Broke Girls 02x08》

一本關於李‧艾默生逃出荊棘崖之後瘋狂連續犯罪的書。

A book about Leigh Emerson and his crime spree after he escaped from Briarcliff.

—— 《American Horror Story 02x12》

✔ 我為什麼不願意走 "You don't think I will."

這句話有反問的口氣，你覺得我不想去嗎？你認為我不會去做嗎？你以為我不想嗎？

→ 你以為，在否定句中的一些用法。

你以為我看不到嗎？

Did you think I wouldn't notice?

—— 《American Horror Story 02x13》

至少現在沒看到那些白癡蝴蝶結了。

Well, at least now you can't see those stupid bows.

你以為我喜歡這些蝴蝶結嗎？／難道你不認為我也討厭這些蝴蝶結嗎？

You don't think I hate the bows?

—— 《*2 Broke Girls 02x05*》

➡ **雙腳攏麻去 "can't feel both my legs"；麻了 "go numb"**

腳麻，my legs go numb [nʌmb] b不發音。

順便記腳麻台語諧音的英文詞彙，kama（性慾／性滿足），Karma（報應／業力）。

因果循環報應不爽真他媽的靈。

Karma can be such a bitch.

—— 《*Femme Fatales 01x01*》

你的沛莉雅會被某個飽讀印度愛經的頭巾男搶跑。

You're gonna lose Priya to some fancy guy in a turban who grew up with Kama Sutra coloring books.

—— 《*The Big Bang 05x02*》

✅ **模仿得不錯 "not a bad job"**

幹的好，在此意指模仿得不錯。模仿，字典上常見的是imitate。口語中常用do impressions當印象或模仿都可以。下例中提到的Michael Hutchence是早期澳洲某搖滾樂團的主唱，97年的時候上吊了。（勇敢求救並非弱者，生命可以找到出路，珍惜生命請您打1995。自動語音 "automated voice"溫馨提示，本服務每分鐘收費一元。）

是你在這裡一直模仿Michael Hutchence。

You're the one going all Michael Hutchence over here.

—— 《Family Guy 09x12 The Hand That Rocks The Wheelchair》

你是要模仿英國口音？

Are you trying to do a British accent?

—— 《Friends 10x03 Ross's Tan》

嘿，兄弟，我們剛剛在玩模仿秀。 你學那個馬歇爾。

Hey, man! We were just doing some impressions. Do your Marcel Marceau.

—— 《Friends 02x14 The Prom Video》

一直被模仿，從未被超越。

Often copied, never equaled.

—— 《Franklin And Bash 02x09》

✔ 我腳痛死了 "my feet are killing me" ；隱隱作痛 "a dull ache"

這篇主要講腳的部分，出門旅遊總是會想多玩多看，腳受累很常見，比如保生大帝廟的行程，要爬一千多階無敵長的樓梯，頭抬起來往上看人都暈了。不說這種比較極端的例子，大部分人久坐辦公室，連續幾天的行程走下來，如果平常少運動的都會有點吃不消，最後再來個大血拚的話，就常聽到類似行程的他團，傳來此起彼落的，「唉唷我的媽呀我的腿呀」，或「哎呀媽呀，我的波棱蓋（東北方言：膝蓋）啊！我的腰間突啊～」。

你的頭怎樣？痛死了。

How's your head? Pretty bad.

—— 《*Stargaze 06x19 The Changeling*》

回聲讓我頭痛死了。

The echo in here is giving me a terrible headache.

—— 《*Get Smart 01x26*》

✅ 簡單省事的例行運動 "a quick and easy workout routine"

睡覺前躺在床上等睡覺無聊的時候，可以做點抬腿運動，雙腳各先緩緩的做10下，然後快速各做50下，過幾天就可以試試100下，不但強壯你的腿，又能瘦小腹，還可助眠 ^^

➡ 跟腳傷走不動有關的一些例句。

我再也走不動了。

I can't walk any more.

—— 《*Skins 05x08*》

我站都站不直，走也走不動。

I couldn't stand. I couldn't walk.

—— 《*Friends 04x01 The Jellyfish*》

穿著蘇菲的大號運動鞋，我根本走不快。

I can't walk any faster in Sophie's giant sneakers.

—— 《*2 Broke Girls 02x05*》

我扭到了腳踝，可能斷了。

I've twisted my ankle. It might be broken.

—— 《Cougar Town 1X21》

但我更高興麗莎扭了腳。

But I'm even happier Lisa sprained her ankle.

—— 《Cougar Town 1x09》

小心。她媽媽會裝腳扭了。

Watch. His mother will fake a sprained ankle.

—— 《Everybody Loves Raymond 07x08 The Annoying Kid》

可樂／可卡因 "coke"

汽水沒氣了或不冰了就不好喝，這汽水沒氣了，The coke has gone flat。Coke的C大寫是指可樂，c小寫是雙關語，有時指可樂，有時指可卡因／古柯鹼 "Cocaine"。

道格，來罐健怡可樂。

Doug, diet Coke?

—— 《House Of Cards 02x09》

我討厭鴉片。是麼，那你的菜是什麼？可卡因？

I hate opium. Oh, yeah, what's your thing? Coke?

—— 《Girls 01x01》

👍 達人提點

✅ 韓國不鏽鋼筷子

好處是，方便切泡菜，韓國人會用筷子把泡菜切成一條一條吃，但是拿不慣的人會覺得這筷子四四角角的又扁又滑，夾菜老是滑掉 "slip out"，特別是肉或菜比較油的，一直夾一直掉，一直夾一直掉，掉到惱羞成怒有沒有。>< |||

把你的手在側面垂下，同時讓槍順勢滑落。
Let your hand drop to your side and let the gun slip out.
—— 《*The Godfather 1972*》

✅ 韓國泡菜

千里迢迢到了這裡 "came all the way here"，別忘了帶點高麗參 "ginseng"，泡菜。雖然有人說酸的泡菜比較健康，但是但是但是我想吃好吃的泡菜啊，不用那啊～麼酸，那啊～麼健康啊，架上賣的某進口韓國泡菜我吃起來一整個就是酸苦。

當你千里迢迢到了賓西法尼亞。
When they drive all the way to Pennsylvania.
—— 《*Everybody Loves Raymond 07X24 Robert's Wedding*》

✅ 韓國泡菜DIY店

這裡的泡菜味道稍微鹹那麼一滴滴，然後沒那麼酸，又香又好吃。這口味跟我念書時的韓國朋友，小華她家媽咪做的一樣正宗 "authentic [ə'θɛn•tɪk]" ^^b順便記 authenticated [ɔ'θɛn•tə•ke•tɪd]（確認無誤的），anesthetic [ˌæ•nəs'θɛ•tɪk]（麻醉藥，麻藥）。

當然，要想做最正宗的，我應該要用鴿子當食材。

Of course, to be truly authentic, I should have made it with pigeon.

—— 《Perception 01x08》

過去九個月，有36起經過證實的類似漢堡航班事故。

In the past nine months, there have been three dozen authenticated incidents like the hamburg flight.

—— 《Fringe 01x01》

✔ Kimchi是專指韓國泡菜

至於一般的泡菜比如臭豆腐裡面那種叫pickled cabbage，榨菜其實也就是四川泡菜 "Sichuan pickled mustard"，酸菜也是醃製的，酸菜如果是芥菜醃的叫Pickled mustard，東北酸菜則是用大白菜 "Chinese cabbage / Chinese leaf" 作的。食材不同。講到大白菜不能不順便記小白菜，pak choi、bok choy，取拼音，東西有同義，反義，對照，相關，聯想性，多比較對照一旦搞清楚了就很容易背起來，還能聯想出一大串。不行再講下去要講不完了，改天有寫美食的英文書再說吧。

2.6

超值韓國
首爾夜景、美容體驗、旅館
之各種想不到

💬 情境對話

 MP3 012

我們提前到達旅館了。
We got to the hotel ahead of time.

路邊一棟中途之家？不是吧？
A roadside halfway house? Seriously?

還好吧。
It's not that bad.

然後我們登記住房了。
Then we'll check in to the hotel.

啥玩意這房間好舊。
What a seedy hotel room.

明天的就會好一點。
We'll have a better lodging tomorrow.

我要另外在別的旅館開房。
I wanna rent a room at another motel.

這個，我可以告訴你那裡有不錯的汽車旅館。
Well, I could tell you where a nice motel is.

公路下就有一個汽車旅館。
There's a motel just down the turnpike.

但是那家的飯難吃得要命。
But the food there stinks.

我比較喜歡這家的早餐。
I'd prefer the breakfast here.

離機場又近，很省時間。
And this hotel is by the airport. It saves us some time.

那隨便吧。
Whatever.

鈴鈴鈴…
Ring Ring Ring...

我沒法吹頭髮。
I can't blow-dry my hair.

吹風機呢？我沒看見有吹風機。
Where is the hair dryer? I don't see a hair dryer around.

而且杯子上有口紅印。
And the glasses have lipstick on them.

馬上就好。
Wait a minute.

815房有位女士需要吹風機。
A lady in Room 815 needs a hair dryer and some glassess.

多久能送過去給她？
When can she get them?

前台
我們立刻送過去。
We'll send them right over.

麥可
謝謝。
Ty. "thank you"

打給房間
316
你的吹風機拿到了嗎？
Did you get your hair dryer?

エリカ
到了，但是…
Yes, but...

エリカ
我本來不想說的，其實浴室也有點臭。
I didn't wanna say anything, but the bathroom smells too.

エリカ
喔喔，這裡有一只蚊子，我們有蚊拍嗎？
Ohohs, there's a mosquito here, do we have a flyswatter?

エリカ
我房間有一只蚊子！聽見嗎？！
There's a mosquito in my room! DO YOU HEAR ME?!

麥可
是的我聽見了。
Yes, I hear you.

麥可
有一瓶殺蟲劑，在房間的桌上。
There is a can of bug spray on the table in the hotel room.

麥可
你要去看一下嗎？
Have you considered looking there?

麥可
還有沒有別的事？我真的該走了，我可以去忙別的了嗎？
Anything else? I should really go now, may I be excused?

エリカ
還有我在浴室跌到了爬不起來。
And I've fallen in the bathroom and I can't get up.

痛不痛？你有受傷嗎？
You hurt? Are you injured?

我的尾椎痛。
My lower back hurts.

你需要醫生。我們坐計程車去。
You need to see a doctor. We'll take a taxi.

我幫你叫計程車。我們去看醫生。
I'll call you a taxi. We'll go see a doctor.

逗你玩的（ㄅㄩㄝ～）。
Ha, got ya. *Tongue out*

讓我屎了吧。你真是夠了。
Kill me. Kill me now.

☆ 單詞與句型

✓ 中途之家 "a roadside halfway house"

A halfway house是指一些中途之家，關懷之家那種的。用在這裡是用來抱怨旅館不滿意，形容旅館差，其實有些旅館雖然舊了一點，但是這方面除了價格考量之外，也要考慮有時旺季或交通地點的問題。旅館除了最常見的hotel、motel，還有其他各種如resort渡假村，lodge（山莊），Inn比較鄉村風的，輕鬆的，字典上説的小旅館，小飯店，小酒館，但現代英語也不一定是這意思了，比如住過一個Holiday Inn就很大一家。最後是介係詞，在旅館用at the hotel，旅館的房間用in the hotel room。

他住在汽車旅館。

He's at the motor lodge.

—《Banshee 02x02》

我放在旅館的桌上…

I had it on the table in the hotel room...

—《Everybody Loves Raymond 06x04 Rays Ring》

接待民宿，一種鄉村旅館，房客通常跟主人住，主人會煮早餐 "B&B: Bed and breakfast"，民宿／青年旅舍 "hostel ['hastl]"，比較便宜，不一定跟主人同住。

寶貝！但千萬別告訴我你是住在青年旅館中的！我可以給你匯錢。

Honey! But please tell me you're not staying in youth hostels. I'm happy to wire you money.

—《Orange Is the New Black 02x01 Thirsty Bird》

✔ 房間好舊 "a seedy hotel room"

貶抑詞，形容破舊的房間。舊有舊的味道，只要乾淨就好，我知道還有些人專門走舊旅館之旅。

那邊實在是太破了。

It was so seedy down there.

—《Mad Men 06x01 02》

今晚，在這破爛的汽車旅館房間裡。

Well, tonight, in this seedy motel room.

—《Femme Fatales 01x05》

我們幹嘛來這個破房子裡啊？

Why are we in this seedy building?

—— 《2 Broke Girls 02x12》

✓ 殺蟲劑 "bug spray"

"bug spray VS. pesticide"：我看pesticides很多翻譯成殺蟲劑，可是中文的殺蟲劑一般是指家裡常見的那種噴蟑螂蚊子螞蟻的，pesticides翻譯成農藥才能跟家中常見的殺蟲劑 "bug spray" 在中文裡有所區別。

悲劇的是，可惡的農藥把蜜蜂殺死了。

Tragically, rogue pesticides. Killed those bees.

—— 《Pushing Daisies 02x01》

我居然帶了兩瓶防蚊液，卻忘了買那個。

I can't believe I brought two cans of bug spray and forgot that.

—— 《Friends 06x22 Where Paul's The Man》

✓ racket

除了球拍之外，也有喧嘩的意思，還有呢，電蚊拍"electric tennis racket"，傳統那種沒電的蒼蠅拍叫 "flyswatter"，不過現在少人用了，多半是用有電的，所以flyswatter你要指電蚊拍也行，口語中不糾結，捕蚊燈跟電蚊拍都可以說bug zapper。我有個電蚊拍來拍死這些蚊子 "I have an electric tennis racket to whack mosquitos."

用蚊子來比喻擊落的敵機，鬧著玩的。

你會在蚊拍上用刻痕計算打死了幾隻蚊子嗎？"Do you put a notch on your flyswatter?" 有些戰鬥機會把擊落的敵機數刻在飛機上，作為一種榮譽跟提振士氣。

蚊子比較少，我用來打蒼蠅跟黃蜂。

Mosquitos are rare, I use it on flies, and wasps.

它會有一種頭髮燒焦的味道說。

It makes a smell like burning hair though.

我倒沒有看著他們的屍體自嗨。

I don't gloat over their demise.

但我有時候把他們曝屍在那裡警告其他蚊子小夥伴 ^^。

But I sometimes leave their corpse out as a warning to the others.

蚊子煩死了特別是在滾床單的時候。

Mosquitoes are annoying especially when you get laid.

✔ 我真的該走了 "I should really go now"

有時我們要走了，又不好意思。或著想表達並不是因為討厭對方才急著離開，後面就會接句話，這句話可能是表達想再跟對方聯絡的意願。

我得走了，電話連絡。

I gotta go. You got my number.

—— 《Cougar Town 1x07》

我得走了，一會兒找你。

I gotta get going. I'll catch you later.

—— 《Cougar Town 1x12》

或接一個理由或爛藉口 "lame excuse" 例如：我該閃了，手機沒電了 "I gotta jet, my cellphone is out of battery." 我有時候會接一些無厘頭的，比如：我必須行動了，這個城市需要我，飛飛飛上天！"I gotta move, this city need me, fly fly fly to the sky!" 你也可以自己想些好玩的 :D

但是我真的得走了。我約了人。

But I have to go. I have a date.

—— 《Burn After Reading》

好爛的藉口。男生的標準答案。

That is a lame excuse. It's a typical guy response.

—— 《Friends 01x18》

✅ 我可以去忙別的了嗎 "may I excuse"

我可以去忙別的了嗎？除了 "I gotta go / run / roll / jet," 不管是當面的離開，或是電話中的離開，就是我們要離開這次對話的意思。May I excuse 是客氣的說我可以去忙別的了嗎？句子越長通常是越客氣，換著不同的話連續表達同樣的意思是表示你的語意越堅持。

我做好了。我正要走呢。

I'm done. I'm just leaving.

—— 《Bones 04x15》

夥計們，我不能再待了。

Guys, I can't be in here.

—— 《2 Broke Girls 02x08》

我走了。

I'm outta here.

—— 《Cougar Town 1x17》

達人提點

✔ 吹頭髮 "blow-dry my hair"；吹風機 "hair dryer"

各式各樣的問題客人都需要你。

✔ 沒熱水 "no hot water"；吹風機壞了 "broken hair dryer"

✔ 浴室排水不良 "the drain problem"

杯緣上有口紅印 "with the lipstick on the rim"

✔ 馬桶不通 "the toilet clogged"；跳電 "black out"

✔ 蚊子咬我 "Mosquitoes bite me."

最難忘的一句是：我沒法睡，我認床 "I can't sleep without my pillow."@@

✔ 前台 "front desk"

有事就找櫃台人員囉 "receptionist / clerk"，他就會叫在店的維修人員過去修，有種110v / 220v的轉換插頭 "outlet switch"，要注意，有些那個圓柱形的鐵的插頭部分太薄太細，如果一般充電碰運氣也許能用，接到熱水壺，電湯匙或高功率的電器產品就會跳電，這類轉換插頭東西建議還是在使用220v的當地買那種比較粗的。

延長線 "an extension cord"

網上看過篇文章說用沒有保險絲的，很粗的那種八爪魚可以直接用，結果有一次在在東南亞某個地方洗完澡準備睡覺怕忘記充電，於是把在日本買的很貴很粗的八爪魚拿出來，一插上不囉嗦直接閃光跳電還冒煙，等旅館維修人員修好之前，房間又黑又燜又熱，我只好開門開窗，接下來就是蚊子小夥伴們在我身上不停的打卡跟按讚，剛才洗澡洗的香噴噴的等於替蚊子洗菜，我用帶血的經驗跟大家說沒必要再試了。還有注意充電器是離開旅館時最容易忘記帶的東西之一，起晚了匆匆忙忙，請各位從房間推出大行李前務必記得詳細檢查每個插座，充電器掉了可惜是一回事，重點在如果充電器不是USB規格的話，有時想借都沒地方借。

無線AP

我的信號滿格 "I got full bars." Wifi很重要有莫有。如果是旅館WiFi推薦可以帶個旅行用迷你無線AP（雲旅機），不大很輕又便宜。旅館的AP不在房間裡也能用。不是那個網上流傳的鋁罐自製WiFi訊號放大器，那自製鋁罐是AP要在你的房間才能這樣用。其實如果AP在你的房間，房間就那麼點大，你也不需要放大器了。我目前用的是DIR-505，如果有什麼好的雲旅機也歡迎跟我分享。

Pocket WiFi

如果是路上也要用WiFi，有一種機器可以租，上網搜下，有些機場也有租WiFi機的服務，比如JAL日航櫃台。

PART 3

台灣好趣處

3.1

讓夢停留
神隱少女、煙雨迷濛的九份

💬 情境對話

MP3 013

麥可：浪漫的，帶點神秘感的，煙雨迷濛的九份。
Jiufen, where romance and the mystery is lost in the fog.

奪目的紅燈籠。
Eye-catching red lanterns.

跟那些深夜裡喧嘩的巷道。
With all that racket in the neighborhood late at night.

沒有看到淘金客的背影，如今只看到如織的遊人了。
You don't see gold miners here anymore, just the tourist crowds all around.

我好像聽到很多人說日語？
I hear a lot of people who are speaking Japanese?

這裡有很多日本觀光客。
We got a lot of Japanese tourists here.

在那裏，阿妹茶樓。有人說好像《神隱少女》裡的場景。
Over there, is the A-Mei Teahouse. Some say it is a scene from Spirited Away.

如果有露天座位的話，你可以喝杯茶享受這景色。
If there's an outdoor seat available, you might wanna have a cup of tea and enjoy the view.

你看那風景，你看。好美！
Look at that scene. Look at that. Gorgeous!

我想說，這地方有種似曾相識的感覺，好像在哪部電影看過？
I mean, it is like a déjà vu. Maybe from some movie?

麥可：嗯，悲情城市，一個1989年得金馬獎的電影。
Yus,《*A City Of Sadness*》, the 1989 Golden Horse Award winner.

就是在九份拍的。
Jiufen is in the movie.

難怪了。
That's why.

這邊有賣什麼東西呢。
What they sell in there?

這裡有各式藝品跟復古玩具。
A variety of crafts and vintage toys.

這裡的禮品店超多。木製明信片是九份的招牌特色。
So many gift shops here. Jiu fen's wooden postcards are well-known.

怎麼這邊好多人在排隊。
Why are so many people lined up over here?

他們有賣什麼？
What do they have?

魚丸跟烤翡翠螺。
Fish balls and roasted Jade whelk.

吃起來什麼味道？
How does it taste?

試試看，吃了就知道。
Give it a shot. See for yourself.

你先吃。
You go first.

這是…天呀！
This is... Holy cow!

就好像我從來沒有吃過魚丸一樣。
It's as if I've never tasted fish balls before.

唇齒留香太好吃了。
That's lip-smacking good.

我也來嚐一口。
Let me have a bite.

是的呀有嚼勁很Q，完美的口感。
Yeah it is chewy and has a perfect texture.

路邊攤快餐的滋味跟口感多半都很豐富。
Street food usually offers a rich variety of tastes and textures.

翡翠羅螺聞起來好香，有一種異國風味。
The Jade whelk smells good. Kind of an exotic flavor.

那是因為五味醬的關係，一種中式海鮮醬。
The secrete is the 5-spice sauce. Chinese call it a kind of seafood sauce.

這些天來我變胖了。
I've put on weight these past few days.

呃？
Eh?

我想我因為這些零食的關係，應該有胖了兩三磅。
I think that I gained two or three pounds on those snacks.

我不覺得耶⋯反正我沒感覺。
I don't think so... I can't tell at all.

麥可，你是最好的領隊了！
Michael, you are the best tour guide ever!

☆ 單詞與句型

✓ 似曾相識 "Deja vu" [dɛ•ʒɑ'vu]

這本來是法語，但是你把他當美語的外來語就好了，類似的例子比如說 Ciao，本來是義大利語，見面打招呼跟再見都能說，美劇裡也常聽到，不過美式的用法一般只有在再見的時候會說。Deja vu是一種似曾相識很微妙的感覺，有人說旅行的時候，可以找到另一個自己，或是發現另一個自己？在加州的某個午後，溫和的陽光在涼涼的空氣中灑下來，一堵白色矮牆後的陰影，兩個小屁孩拿塊石頭蹲地上畫圖，聽到媽咪喊吃飯了去洗手，慌慌張張的扔了石頭又推又鬧地與你擦身而過一路跑回家，這時候，你有感覺到心裡的某個角落動了一下嗎？It is like a deja vu。

你有過似曾相識的感覺嗎？某一刻的當下覺得好像之前在哪裡曾經經歷過。

Have you ever had deja vu? Living a moment you've already lived before.

—— 《Fringe 01x20》

似曾相識其實就是－就是－就是另一個人生的匆匆一瞥。幾乎每個人都會有所經歷。

Deja vu is--is--is simply a-a momentary glimpse to the other side. Almost everyone experiences it.

我們覺得我們好像曾經去過某個地方。這是因為我們在平行宇宙裡的確去過。

We feel that we've been somewhere before. Because actually we have in another reality.

—— 《Fringe 01x19》

✓ 名產／特產／土產／招牌特色／拿手好菜／強項 "specialty / specialties"

本店的特色。
Specialty of the house.

—— 《Arrow 01x11》

破解密文是我的一項拿手好戲。
Decoding the secret messages are one of my specialties.

—— 《Get Smart 01x28》

今天是集市日，鎮上熙熙攘攘，所有東西都是新鮮的當地土產-當季貨。

It's market day, and the city's jammed. Everything is fresh and local - so seasonal.

—— 《*Rick Steves Europe Frances Dordogne 2008*》

我以為你們是海豹突擊隊戰友？他的強項是什麼？

I thought you guys were Navy SEALs? What was his specialty?

—— 《*Hawaii Five O 01x09*》

✔ 變胖 "put on weight" ；胖了兩三磅 "gained two or three pounds"

我真的那麼顧人怨嗎？每次我稍微變胖時，我都會胡思亂想。

Am I hideously ['hɪdiəslɪ] unattractive? Every time I put on a little weight. I question everything.

—— 《*Friends 02x07 Ross Finds Out*》

如果我變胖了，你會跟我分手嗎？

Will you break up with me if I get fat?

—— 《*Friends 07x06 The Nap Partners*》

吃了太多高熱量的雞翅，很快的糖尿病、肥胖症和夜盲症就接踵而來。

Diabetes, obesity, and night blindness were all quick to follow the coated volumes of wings.

—— 《*Pushing Daisies 02x08*》

put on活用：除了長胖變胖用 "put on weight" 之外，中文裡的穿（衣服）戴（帽子），英文都是用put on。穿上西裝 "put on a suit"，戴帽子戴手

套 "put on your hat and gloves"。put on跟air一起用是擺架子的意思，他從不擺架子 "He never put on airs"，那跟face一起用呢？他板著臉，擺著臭臉"He put on a straight face"，擺張樸克臉"He put on a poker face."。put on還有一些其他的用法：

邦德先生你的演技不錯。

Mr. Bond. You put on a good show.

——《007 Skyfall 2012》

繫好安全帶，閣下。

Put on your seat belt, sir.

——《Arrow 01x01》

孩子們，大家都帶上護目鏡吧。

Okay, kids, everybody put on their goggles ['gagls]。（看成google的舉手！ ^^!

——《Bones 04x11》

來些飲料怎麼樣，再加上音樂？

How about some drinks, put on some music?

——《Everybody Loves Raymond 07x02 Counseling》

✓ 露天 "outdoor"

你打赤膊參加一個露天派對。

You show up shirtless to an outdoor party.

——《How I Met Your Mother 07x08》

漫遊格林威治村的露天巴士。

Open-air buses that drive around the West Village.

—— 《*The Newsroom 01x10*》

✅ 露天建築物

旅遊經常會遇到露天的各種地方。這方面一些線上字典寫得很亂，幫大家做個簡單的整理，並列出比較代表性的例句。想像自己站在屋頂上，以房子為中心，由上而下，由近到遠，由大到小，這類東西的介系詞差不多都全部用on。

陽台 "balcony ['bæl•kə•nɪ]"。我們常說的陽台，看風景，放點盆栽的地方或歌劇院的包廂。頂樓陽台 "penthouse balcony"；屋頂陽台、大陽臺 "Terrace ['tɛ•rəs]"。

門廊 "porch [pɔr•tʃ]"。給家人留一盞回家的燈 "the porch light"。

戶外的，露天的 "alfresco [æl'frɛs•ko]"。作形容詞是在戶外，在露天，澳洲英語你可以把它當作patio，有些做的比較浪漫精緻。

開放式空間 "patio ['pæ•tɪo]"。這個字比較籠統，有時指小前院的alfresco，有時指大中庭，加個roof，roof patio又等同terrace。

帳篷，涼亭 "gazebo [gə'zɪ•bo]"。有些硬式固定結構的像個涼亭，有輕便的像個帳篷。

✅ 我們常說的陽台，"balcony ['bæl•kə•nɪ]" 頂樓陽台 "penthouse balcony"

瞧陽台這扇拉門！

Look at the balcony with the sliding doors!

—— 《*Everybody Loves Raymond 3x09 The Lone Barone*》

我看過了你設計的頂樓陽台。

I looked at your design for the penthouse balcony.

—— 《How I Met Your Mother x Aldrin Justice》

她在屋頂露台發現，理查抽過的雪茄。

She found one of Richard's cigar butts on the terrace.

—— 《Friends 03x01 The Princess Leia Fantasy》

門廊 "porch [pɔr•tʃ]"

給家人留一盞回家的燈，通常就是the porch light。

還會一直開著門廊燈，等她回心轉意。

Even kept the porch light on in case she changed her mind, you know.

—— 《Hawaii Five 03x15》

門廊前還有斜坡。

A ramp on the front porch.

—— 《Shameless Us 2x07 》

戶外的，露天的 "alfresco [æl'fr ɛ s•ko]"

澳洲英語就把它當作類似名詞patio。

熊熊營火，喝上兩杯，來個星光炒飯。

Camp fires, booze, alfresco sex.

—— 《Skins 02x04 Michelle》

開放式空間 "patio ['pæ•tɪo]"

這個字比較籠統，就是個有些陳設可以休憩的開放式空間，有時指前院的alfresco，the backyard patio指後院的alfresco。有時指大中庭，加個roof，變成roof patio當作terrace。

我聽說會設計一個可愛的頂樓露台。

I hear there's a lovely rooftop patio.

　　　　　　　—— 《*How I Met Your Mother 6x05 Architect Of Destruction*》

在中庭享受雞尾酒。

Cocktails on the patio.

　　　　　　　—— 《*How I Met Your Mother 6x18 A Change Of Heart*》

帳篷，涼亭 "gazebo [gə'zɪ•bo]"

有些硬式固定結構的像個涼亭，有輕便的像個帳篷。

有小孩藏在露台底下！

There's babies hiding under the gazebo!

　　　　　　　—— 《*Girls 01x04*》

 達人提點

風景很美的幾種說法

千山萬水，全靠導遊一張嘴，很美除了那一句臭酸的very beautiful，既然身為導覽人員，我們要來多練幾句關於風景的相關說法，這裡風景很迷人"Great view"；"Nice spot; The view here is amazing." 你看那風景"Look at that view." 我要去看風景 "I'm gonna see the sights."

外面景色很美。

It's beautiful out.

—— 《Bobs Burgers 01x12》

房頂可以一覽浪漫美景。

The roof has a very romantic view.

—— 《Be Wtih You 01x02》

✔ 我在欣賞風景

欣賞用 "admire" 這個字，"I am admiring the view." 是不是比講 "I am looking at the view." 感覺更爽？有種讚嘆造物者的鬼斧神工那味道，欣賞了然後怎麼樣，順勢沉醉一下，我沉醉其中 "I basked in the awesomeness."

風景看夠了，來看看這個。

That's enough of the view, check this out.

—— 《Friends 01x15》

不想浪費這麼好的景色，不想錯過這美景。

Hate to waste a view.

—— 《007 Skyfall 2012》

3.2

台灣好遊趣
中正紀念堂、帥哥操槍
超吸睛

 MP3 014

💬 情境對話

麥可

接下來，我們參觀中正紀念堂跟操槍表演。
Next, we'll visit Chiang Kai-shek Memorial Hall and watch the changing of the guards exhihition drill.

麥可

你可以靠近一點。
You can come closer.

YoYoKo

哇！他們的兩臂貼緊，站的好筆直。
Wow! Their arms are at their side, as straight as a pencil.

YoYoKo

好多遊客聚在廣場圍觀儀式啊。
So many tourists pack the square to witness the exhibition.

麥可

對啊，這裡人好多。
Yes. There are a lot of people here.

麥可

這是台灣著名的觀光景點之一，所以這裡的人潮總是很多。
This is one of the most famous spots in Taiwan, so there are tourists here all day.

麥可

你可以再走近他們一點。
It's okay if you want to step a little closer to them.

為什麼禮兵的制服顏色不一樣？
Why are those uniforms different colors?

三軍各有他們自己的制服。
Every branch of the military ['mɪlɪtɛrɪ] has their own uniforms.

白色的是海軍，綠色的是陸軍，藍色的是空軍。
White for Navy, green for Army, blue for Air Force.

可以幫我隨便拍幾張嗎？
Could you do me a favor and take my picture?

樂意之至。
With pleasure.

笑一個，説瑜珈！
Smile, say YOGA!

摩卡！
MOCHA!

盡量多拍幾張。好嗎？
Take as many as you want. Okay?

沒問題。
You got it.

好了這邊走。我們去樓上看看。
All right this way. Let's check out upstairs.

這是誰啊？
Who is this?

那是蔣介石的銅像。
That is the statue ['stætʃu] of Chiang Kai Shek.

麥可

大家在這裡隨便逛逛，然後我們下樓。
Feel free to take a look around, and then we can go downstairs.

麥可

這兩旁是劇院跟音樂廳。
There is a theatre ['θiətə] and a concert hall on the sides.

麥可

不過這次我們的行程沒有包含看表演。
But unfortunately, there's no performance to watch in our itinerary this trip.

YoYoKo

有一天我會再回來，也許若干年後吧。
I'll be back again, probably in a couple years from now.

YoYoKo

我肚子好餓，餓死了。嘿，麥可，今天晚上吃什麼？
I'm hungry. Actually, starving. Hey, Michael, what's for dinner?

麥可

我們看看喔…我的行程表上是寫…韓式泡菜火鍋。
Let's see... My itinerary [aɪ'tɪ•nə•rɛ•rɪ] says... Kimchi hot pot.

YoYoKo

又一樣？昨晚就跟你說我最討厭火鍋了。
Again? I told you I hated hot pot last night.

麥可

就兩天，明天吃烤肉了。
Just two days in a row. We have a BBQ Block Party tomorrow.

YoYoKo

那還不是一樣，今天還是要吃火鍋。
Isn't that kind a similar, so hot pot again tonight.

YoYoKo

這團好爛，每天吃火鍋。
This tour group sucks. We eat hot pot every day.

麥可

不想理你。
Talk to the hand.

YoYoKo

喂！我是人客ㄟ。
Psst! I am your CUSTOMER.

麥可

行。投降。
Okey. YOU WIN.

☆ 單詞與句型

✔ 操槍表演 "the exhibition drill"

Armed Drill也行，"dance drill / cheerleading" 是大家熟悉的手上拿著兩坨pompon（啦啦球）的啦啦隊。cheerleader有常被以為是啦啦隊長，其實是全體啦啦隊員，lead是帶動觀眾領導觀眾的意思。那啦啦隊長怎麼說呢？加個頭 "head cheerleader" 就是啦。

不，不過我確實追過啦啦隊所有人。
No, no, but I, uh, I did chase all the cheerleaders.

—— 《Hawaii Five O 02x13》

我還得參加啦啦隊訓練呢。
I have cheerleading practice.

—— 《How I Met Your Mother 07x12》

✔一般說表演，用act、show就可以了，performance也行。

我們的表演沒有這部分，各位。

This is not part of the show, people.

—— 《Bobs Burgers 01x05》

觀看表演。

See the act.

—— 《Boardwalk Empire 1x06 Family Limitation》

各位，這是最後一場演出了。

Final performance, people.

—— 《Bobs Burgers 01x05》

✔效率，表演 "performance"

這個要用點想像力，效率，表演…辛苦練習後漂亮的演出？

腰墊能提高我的工作效率。

Lumbar ['lʌmbɚ] support could enhance my job performance.

—— 《Bones 04x06》

✔人好多，好多人 "a lot of people, a big crowd"

好多人大半夜會看電視呢。

Plenty of people are watching TV in the middle of the night.

—— 《Mind Games S1x02》

我以前很容易怯場。

I was terrified about appearing in front of a big crowd.

—— 《The Big Bang 03x18》

✅ 樂意之至 "with pleasure"

人家請你幫忙時，常需要回答樂意之至，我的榮幸，這類的話。你可以
簡單說pleasure，a pleasure或007詹姆士龐德酷酷的with pleasure，比
祖傳的It's my pleasure更casual，anytime或everything也很親切。

我很樂意。

I'm happy to.

—— 《*2 Broke Girls 1x21 And The Messy Purse Mackdown*》

樂意之至。

I'd be delighted.

—— 《*Chicago Pd 01x03*》

兩位探員大駕光臨，榮幸之至。

Detectives. My gracious.

—— 《*American Horror Story 02x04*》

✅ 那如果想主動幫忙呢？

如果有什麼我可以效勞的⋯

If there's anything I can do...

—— 《*Boardwalk Empire 1x03 Broadway Limited*》

有什麼我可以為你們效勞的嗎？

So what can I do for you boys?

—— 《*Hawaii Five O 03x23*》

✅ 為您效勞

對大人講這種口氣，嗯…看人看場合氣氛也許偶一為之。對小朋友就還蠻好玩的，比如：

聽候你的差遣，小可愛。

I'm at your service, adorable.

—— 《*Game Of Thrones 01x02*》

安安，請吩咐，夫人。（前後夾兩句義大利語，帶點異國風唷。）
Buongiorno, at your service, signora.

—— 《*The Godfather 1990*》

任何事都願為您效勞，小姑娘。

Anything for you, cutie pie :D

—— 《*Hot In Cleveland 04x08 Extras*》

✅ 若干年後 "years from now"

如果沒有説幾年，那就是若干年後，如果有清楚説幾年，那就是幾年後。

而我這三十年後會做些什麼呢？

What am I gonna be doing 30 years from now?

—— 《*Cougar Town 1x06*》

誰會在乎20年後的日子？

Okay who cares about 20 years from now?

—— 《*Cougar Town 1x13*》

沒錯，再過不到十年吧，當我把他改造成功以後。

Oh yeah in about ten years from now, when I'm done changing him.

—— 《Cougar Town 1x13》

火鍋 "fondue, hot pot"

火鍋除了說hot pot，也可以說Chinese fondue，fondue [fan'du]，放毒？放心沒有毒的，fondue是歐洲那種用起士或巧克力為底，或肉類為底（Meat Fondue）的小火鍋，瑞士著名的美食。沒有吃過豬肉，也看過豬跑步，有時跟老外解釋一些東西，可以用他們本身就熟悉的詞彙再去加以變化跟解釋，比如Chinese fondue。相對來說，中文也有類似這樣的用法，有些東西沒有中文名稱，但是跟既有的東西類似，就會取個美國什麼的名字，比如類固醇很好用，中文裡治百病的就叫仙丹，所以類固醇又叫美國仙丹。

艾米，火鍋太棒了！

Amy, kudos on the fondue!

—— 《Everybody Loves Raymond 09x13》

Claire和Austin剛剛邀請我們去參加他們的乳酪火鍋宴。

Claire and Austin just invited us to their fondue fest.

—— 《How I Met Your Mother 01x05 Okay Awsome》

你們在聊什麼，艾米？ 火鍋之夜。

What were you talking about, Amy? Fondue date night.

—— 《Everybody Loves Raymond 09x13》

烤肉 "BBQ"

如果喜歡吃燒烤的，可以上網蒐烤霸 "Pitmasters"，美國有名的BBQ風格大多是來自於中西部或南方。一年一度的Big Apple BBQ Block Party，於每年六月的第一個週末，在紐約市的麥迪遜廣場 "Madison Square Park" 舉辦，美國各地的Pitmaster來此競技，不用走遍整個美國，就可以吃透透各種不同風格的BBQ，性價比"C／P"非非非常高，內行人的選擇 ^^。

歡迎來到週末烤肉！我帶了啤酒和番茄醬。

Welcome to barbecue Saturday! I brought a six-pack and some ketchup.

—— 《Cougar Town 1x07》

我終於可以在空氣流通的地方烤東西了。

I'm finally gonna be able to barbecue with proper ventilation [ˌvent'leʃn].

—— 《How I Met Your Mother 07x08》

美國南方

"Tell me about yourself dude, west coast, or east?" 新來的兄弟報下三圍戶口，東岸還是西岸的？這句常聽，但是美國除了分東西岸，還有第三岸嗎？Dirty South就是the 3rd coast第三岸。"I am from the Dirty South." 哥打傷不起的南方來的，"This is how we roll in the Dirty South!" 在南方我們就是這麼玩的！寫這篇的時候我正在聽這首歌，影片網站搜下這五個英文字 "Dirty South Until The End" 會有驚喜喔，聽聽歌 "Just let you go till the end of time it's you and I." 雖然你我相忘於地老天荒，但忘不掉Dirty South的Fu了 :D

✅ 每天 "every day"

every day是時間副詞。

古怪的你是那麼的迷人。和你在一起的每一天都像是一次探險。
You're so wonderfully weird. Every day with you is an adventure.

—— 《Friends 10x12 Phoebe's Wedding》

比較 everyday是形容詞或名詞。形容詞如：日常生活中 "In everyday life"，在我們的日常生活中 "in our everyday lives"，一本常用片語書 "an everyday phrases book"。名詞如：全年無休 "Everyday 24 / 7"，讀做 everyday twenty-four seven。

我是巴尼‧史汀森醫生。你的傲人上圍是否大到讓日常生活都困難重重呢？
I'm Dr. Barney Stinson. Are your really large breasts making everyday tasks difficult?

—— 《How I Met Your Mother 07x04》

✅ 不想理你 "Talk to the hand"

去跟你的手說話別跟我說，就是不要煩我了。我無視你了，懶得理你，I'm just ignoring you。在美劇《2 Broke Girls》中，餐廳老闆的名字Han（中譯阿憨），音似hand，所以才有了以下這個笑點：

懶得理你阿憨！
Talk to the Han!

—— 《2 Broke Girls 1x05 And The 90S Horse Party》

👍 達人提點

✅ 嚴重聲明

我要在此感謝我所有帶過的貴賓，並表示我帶過的都是最好的客人！好人客的鼓勵讓我們工作的更有熱忱，機智的客人讓我們帶團 "running a tour" 的經驗更豐富！ ^^|||

這就是你的待客之道嗎？

This is how you greet guests?

—— 《Friends 01x10》

他不過就是個耍流氓的客人。

He's just a customer that went rogue.

—— 《2 Broke Girls 01x07 And The Pretty Problem》

剛才是一個凹客，不是咩？

That was a sneaky customer, now wasn't it?

—— 《2 Broke Girls 01x13 And The Secret Ingredient》

✅ 借廁所

我們的洗手間只供我們的客人使用 "Our rest rooms are for our customers only." 有些熱門景點的餐廳咖啡廳廁所只限有消費的客人使用，廁所門上密碼鎖的密碼會在你點餐的收據上。

3.3

花園夜市上
臉書打卡熱門景點台灣
稱冠、全球總排行12

💬 情境對話

MP3 015

麥可

唷吼吼～各位貴賓，是時候起床了唷。
Yo ho ho~ guys, time to wake up.

Carolyn

我們到花園夜市了嗎？
Are we at the night market?

麥可

是的。到處都是色香味俱全，誘人的小吃喔。
Yup. Delicious displays and tempting eateries everywhere.

麥可

貴重物品留在車上。下巴士的時候請大家注意台階。
Leave your valuables in the car. Watch your step please when you get off the bus.

麥可

請別忘了我們的車牌號碼是CB-868。
Please notice that the plate number is CB eight sixty eight.

Carolyn

所以待會我們集合的地點就在這裡嗎？
So later we'll meet up right here?

麥可

對，你可以在這個路口拍張照。
Right, you might wanna take a photo of the intersection.

這裡人潮非常的多，萬一你走失了，把手機上拍的照片給店家看。
There's a lot of foot traffic here. If you get lost, show the photo you took to vendors.

麥可

不要問路人。他們可能也是觀光客，他們也不知道。
Don't ask a random person walking by for directions. They could be a tourist just like you. They won't know any better.

麥可

或者你留在原地不動，我會去找你。
Or just stay put. I'll come to you.

麥可

我們下次集合的時間是八點整。
We'll meet back up here at 8:00 p.m. sharp.

麥可

現在請跟著我走，走囉出發囉！
Walk with me, heeeere We Go!

麥可

你有特別想要吃什麼嗎？
Are you craving for anything?

麥可

我一整個沒概念…
I have no idea...

Carolyn

額滴媽呀那味道是哪裡來的？
Mamamiya where is that smell coming from?

Carolyn

咳咳，那是臭豆腐，衷心希望你能嘗一口。（奸笑）
Ahem, that is fermented tofu, I hope that you will taste it. *evil grin*

麥可

謝謝再連絡，然後那個是什麼？雞肉？
Thanks, but no, thanks and what is that? Chicken?

Carolyn

麥可
對啊，那是鹹水雞。
Yup, that is brined chicken with pepper.

 Carolyn
我要試那個，你推薦配什麼青菜呢？麥可。
I will try that, what veggies do you recommend? Michael.

 麥可
它跟青花椰，四季豆，豆皮很搭。
It goes with broccoli, string beans, and especially Bean curd sheets.

 Carolyn
什麼是豆皮？它吃起來像臭豆腐嗎？
What are bean curd sheets? Do they taste like fermented tofu?

 麥可
它們是表兄弟，但是味道不一樣。
They are cousins, but they taste different.

 Carolyn
好，我試一下好了，祝我幸運。
Okay, I will give it a shot, wish me luck.

 麥可
小辣、中辣、大辣。
Mild, medium, or spicy.

 Carolyn
那麼就…中辣？
Then... Medium?

 麥可
好，來給你。
Okay, here you go.

 Carolyn
豆皮好吃。我想我可以試試它的表兄弟，你剛說叫啥？
The bean curd sheets taste good. I think I can try their cousin, what was that again?

 麥可
臭豆腐。你值得擁有。
Fermented tofu. You know you want it.

Carolyn
很好，那你推薦什麼湯呢？
Great, what soup do you recommend?

麥可
青蛙湯。
Frog soup.

Carolyn
不好意思？什麼湯來著？
Excuse me? What soup again?

麥可
青蛙湯跟臭豆腐很配，養顏美容的秘訣。
Frog soup goes good with fermented tofu. It is the secret to a great complexion.

Carolyn
慢著，真的嗎？不你不是說真的。
Wait, seriously? NO, you are NOT serious.

☆ 單詞與句型

✓ 是時候 "time to"

是時候起床了。

Time to wake up.

該上巴士了。

Time to get on the bus.

該睡覺了。

Time to hit the sack.

☑ 下巴士 "get off the bus"

下車有很多種講法，比較大型的，載客數多的如："bus / train / airplane / ship"這些交通工具，用 "on / off"；比較小型的如："car / taxi"的話，用 "in / out"。**例如** "get in the car / get out of the car"。

我終於要上飛機啦。麥克斯，你沒坐過飛機嗎？

I am finally going a plane ride. Max, you've never been on a plane?

—— 《2 Broke Girls 02x16》

我不敢相信你竟然買了這車。載我一程吧，猛男？跳上車。

I can't believe you bought this. So can I have a ride, stud? Hop in.

—— 《Friends 07x14 Where They All Turn Thirty》

"in / out"也可以用在人身上但意思是妨礙，**例如** 好狗不擋路"Out of my way / get out of my way / Don't get in my way"。下面這句很形象，識相的自己走出去，要不把你從窗戶扔出去：

好狗不擋路滾出去，別敬酒不吃吃罰酒。

Better door than window.

—— 《Shameless Us 01x02》

☑ 車牌號碼 "plate number"

車牌是plate或license plate，要念abcd也行，有時念這種a-alpha，b-bravo，比較清楚，尤其在電話中或戶外風大人多吵雜的地方，航空代碼 "the aviation [ˌe•vɪ'e•ʃən] / pilot's / army alphabet"：

- A - Alpha ['æl•fɑ]   N - November [no'vɛm•bɚ]
- B - Bravo ['brɑˌvo]   O - Oscar ['ɑs•kɚ]

- C - Charlie [ˈtʃɑr•lɪ]
- D - Delta [ˈdɛl•tə]
- E - Echo [ˈɛ•ko]
- F - Foxtrot [ˈfɔks•trɔt]
- G - Golf [gɑlf]
- H - Hotel [hoˈtɛl]
- I - India [ˈɪn•dɪˈɑ]
- J - Juliet [ˈdʒu•lɪˈɛt]
- K - Kilo [ˈkɪlo]
- L - Lima [ˈlaɪ•mɑ]
- M - Mike [maɪk]

P - Papa [ˈpɑpəpəˈpɑ]
Q - Quebec [kuɪˈbɛk]
R - Romeo [ˈro,mɪo]
S - Sierra [sɪˈɛ•rɑ]
T - Tango [ˈtæŋ•go]
U - Uniform [ˈju•nɪ,fɔrm]
V - Victor [ˈvɪk•tə]
W - Whiskey [ˈhwɪs•kɪ]
X - X-ray [,ɛksˈre]
Y - Yankee [ˈjæŋ•kɪ]
Z - Zulu [ˈzu•lu]

✅ 萬一你走失了 "what if you lost"

迷路可以説You Are Lost？You Got Lost？Get Lost另外有叫人滾蛋的意思，如果怕搞不清楚那就用are，或乾脆把are或get省略掉在口語中也沒事。

這裡很容易迷路。
It's really easy to get lost in here.

—— 《*Hawaii Five O 02x07*》

我們好像有點迷路了。
We seem to be a little bit lost.

—— 《*How I Met Your Mother 03x02 We Are Not From Here*》

看來他是走錯路了。
Looks like he went the wrong way.

—— 《*Pushing Daisies 02x12*》

✅ 留在原地不動 "stay put"

比stay There更強調原地不動，萬一迷路，你不動人家就容易找你，想像那個畫面，兩個人都走動就比較難遇到了。

我們會去找你，你待在原地。我們這就過去。
We'll find you. Stay put. We're on our way.

—— 《Homeland 02x10》

✅ 我會去找你 "I'll come to you"

如果是you，用come to you。如果用go to，常聽到是接 your "house／place／party"。

那我搬去你那裡然後你和湯姆一起住好了。
Then I'll go to your place and you can move in with Tom.

—— 《The Talented Mr Ripley》

我會去參加你的蘇格蘭羊雜宴會。
I'll go to your haggis party.

—— 《The Big Bang 04x17》

✅ 出發囉 "heeeere we go"

here加長音，很多學英語的人在網上找老外聊，這樣很簡單的就可以適當的加進語感，聊起來比較自然喔。路邊小吃 "street food／snack"，但如果用street delights這樣有沒有感覺更好吃呢？*wink*

河邊整排都是流行的小吃。
The river's lined with trendy eateries.

—— 《Rick Steves Europe Denmark Beyond Copenhagen》

他就在小吃攤旁邊。

He's near the food vendors.

—《Hawaii Five O 02x21》

✓ 你有特別想要 "are you craving for"

有特別想要…嗎？提到吃的東西或點菜時，經常會問到人的喜好，比如，辣度可依個人喜惡而調整，參考以下幾種表達的方式：

我去拿你的菜。

I'll get you your usual.

—《2 Broke Girls 02x18》

都按你喜歡的樣子切好了，心肝寶貝。

All cut up like you like, sweetheart.

—《Everybody Loves Raymond 03x05 The Visit》

我撒上的全都是你喜歡的配料。

I'll make it with all the toppings you like.

—《Be Wtih You 01x08》

是嗎，辣度如何？ 辣度正好。

Yeah? How is the spiciness of it? That's just the right amount of spice.

—《Chinese Food Made Easy 01x05》

我喜歡當我的興趣和工作結合的時候。

I love it when my personal desires are the same as my professional duties.

—《Secret Diary Of A Call Girl 01x02》

臭豆腐 "fermented tofu"

發酵過的豆腐，就是臭豆腐，介紹美食，有時這個用詞方面，不建議說 stinky tofu。攤販 "vendor"，他有個攤子。pedlar是脖子上掛個籃子走來走去叫賣的小販，意思略有不同。

謝謝再連絡 "Thank, but no, thanks"

事緩則圓，有時說等一下就是永遠等一下了意同拒絕 "Sometimes we say later, we know that might mean never." 如果不直接說No是一種藝術，那該說No的時候就是一種智慧了。加上點擬聲詞"No. Uh-uh."不，不行不可以。

他們知道適時地拒絕。

They knew when to say no.

—— 《24Hrs 08x09》

開誠佈公地說，不行。

Opening dialogue ['daɪəlɔg] No.

—— 《2 Broke Girls 02x05》

你想都不用想了，不用白花心思了。

Don't get any ideas.

—— 《2 Broke Girls 02x01》

不要迷戀我。

Don't get attached.

—— 《2 Broke Girls 01x01 Pilot》

✅ 小辣中辣大辣 "mild medium or spicy"

日常生活中，我們常說的大辣中辣小辣，還有不辣要怎麼說呢？除了說 no chili，又多一個方式表達不辣，去掉no加上please，"Please hold the chili pepper."是不是感覺不一樣呢？

→ 無敵辣。

吃過鬼椒嗎？我第一次挖辣椒的時候是用湯匙，第二次以後就改用牙籤了^^有些形容方式就是講的誇張點比較好玩，也讓你的英文更加生動活潑。形容極辣可以試試以下的說法：辣椒在嘴巴里掃射 "explosively hot"，辣爆頭 "literally blow your head off"，超辣 "very hottest / extra spicy"。

- 大辣 "hot / fiery / spicy"
- 中辣 "medium / medium spicy"
- 小辣 "mild / mild chili"
- 微辣 "very mildest"
- 不辣 "please hold the chili."

👍 達人提點

✅ 點整 "sharp"

Eight o'clock你高興的話也可以念作zero eight hundred。差不多八點 "right about eight o'clock"，**例如** 我總是在晚上讀故事書給她聽然後在8點左右哄她入睡 "I read her a book and tuck her in right about 8:00." 客人沒有不遲到的，有時也不是故意的，但是還是要注意其他不遲到的客人的感覺，如果某組客人老是遲到，其他人可能會有點…覺得不公平？
這時就要靠你的經驗與智慧去拿捏分寸。團體出遊當然希望客人能守
時，但是説的時候不要忘了臉上的微笑跟口氣的尊重喔 ^^

✅ 各種特殊餐食 "SPML"

比如素食，兒童餐，嬰兒餐"BBML, babymeal"，水果餐，上飛機前就要
確定，如果領隊有重新劃位，別忘了告知辛苦的空姐，免得造成她們送
餐的困擾。通常在行前説明會或行程表都會提醒，如果有這方面需求的
客人，可自行帶些素食罐頭或泡麵。吃素還有分：

✅ 吃方便素的人 "A flexitarian [ˌflɛk•sə'tɛ•rɪən]"

方便素又稱鍋邊素，桌邊素。吃方便素的人大部份都是因為健康因素吃
素，而不是宗教因素。如出門在外或跟朋友一起吃飯的時候，即使葷素
煮在一起，只要挑出素的吃即可，而不用考慮鍋子是否有沾到葷的。

✅ 素食者／蔬菜／青菜 "veggie"

這有兩個意思，可以是vegetables（蔬菜）或vegetarian（素食者）。吃
菜日，veggie day，如初一十五拜拜吃素。 例如 素食漢堡更健康
"Veggie is healthier."

✅ 吃純素／蛋奶素 "vegan ['vɪ•gən]"

連蛋奶都不吃。vegan是一種信念主張盡可能地避免虐待動物。稱呼這種
人的話，説 "He is a vegan person." 比説 "He is a vegan." 好。

3.4 花園夜市下 烤雞炸雞夾娃娃機

💬 情境對話

MP3 016

Carolyn
還有什麼特別出名的小吃？
Any other specialties ['spɛ•ʃl•tɪs] ?

麥可
蚵仔麵線，吃貝類會過敏嗎？
Oyster vermicelli, do you have a shellfish allergy?

Carolyn
海鮮類？我會過敏。
Seafood? I have a sensitivity.

麥可
那章魚燒呢？恩…當我沒說。
How about octopus fritters? Hmm... Forget it.

麥可
也許你對海鮮過敏，還是別自找麻煩好。
Maybe you are allergic to seafood. It's an necessary risk.

Carolyn
你會對什麼過敏嗎？麥可。
Are you allergic to something? Michael.

麥可
我對胡蘿蔔過敏。
I am allergic to carrots.

Carolyn
屁啦，沒有人對胡蘿蔔過敏，我不信。
Crap, no one is allergic to carrots. I don't buy it.

麥可
愛信不信。欸…你看！
Believe what you want. Eh... Look!

麥可
青蛙下蛋，西米露，愛玉，仙草，都有耶，挺好的。
Tapioca bubbles, sago soup, fig jelly, herb jelly, check check check.

Carolyn
我想吃咔啦烤雞。
I miss battered fried chicken.

麥可
抱歉，這個沒辦法有。
Sry "sorry," No can do.

麥可
只有咔啦炸雞，炸的，不是烤的。
We've got crispy chicken here, deep fried, not oven baked.

麥可
你喜歡甜食還是鹹食？
Do you prefer sweet or savoury food?

Carolyn
隨便啊都可以 ^^Y
I could go either way.

謎之音))) 阿喜上身？最怕聽到這種答案有木有了～ "Miss cranky pants've gotten into you? This is the last thing you want to hear about~"

Carolyn
喔喔，那是什麼？
Ooh ooh, what's that?

麥可
炸蟋蟀，我不覺得你會喜歡。
Fried crickets ['krɪ•kɪ•ts] , I don't think you're going to like them.

Carolyn
你吃過嗎？
Have you ever had them?

麥可
我嚐過，稀世珍品人間美味。
I've tasted them. This is divine.

Carolyn
救人啊幫幫忙！
Yikes!

麥可
不吃是你的損失，我照樣頭好壯壯。
Your loss. I'm awesome.

麥可
你可以看看那個滷味。很下酒。
You might wanna try that Fragrant Chinese stew. It's good with booze.

謎之音
媽媽以後再也不用擔心我會說出滷味是Chinese-style soy sauce braised pot stewed dishes這種英文了 :D

Carolyn
紅酒配滷味？
A red wine with that Chinese stew?

麥可
嗯…我向您推薦啤酒。
Hum... I recommend beer.

Carolyn
這裡人很多。
It is crowded here.

麥可
人多熱鬧。
The more, the merrier.

Carolyn
看看這些便宜小玩意兒…在那裡！有夾娃娃機！
Look at these cheap gadgets. Over there! A bear claw machine!

麥可
有硬幣嗎？
You have any coins?

Carolyn

嗯有。
Yep.

Carolyn

回來了。我真的變拚的。
I'm back. I'm really tried.

Carolyn

花了10分鐘在那台死夾娃娃機，想抓出來那隻袋鼠。
Ten minutes on the damn claw machine, trying to get the kangaroo.

Carolyn

不過最後還是只夾到了這只棒棒糖。
But all I could get was this lollipop.

☆ 單詞與句型

✓ 蚵仔麵線 "oyster vermicelli"

Vermicelli是一種義大利細麵條，比大家熟知的義大利麵Spaghetti要細。翻成Oyster thin noodles也沒什麼不對。這個英文翻譯還不算長，有時候翻譯美食的時候，最常見的問題就是會變的又臭又長，比如5個字的乾煸四季豆變成Dry-Fried French Beans with Minced Pork and Preserved Vegetables，上面這還是北京奧運中英菜單找出來的，雖然句子長但還有意思在，有些翻譯只是失控的一大長串。所以如果vermicelli可以讓老外理解，就可以請這些有完沒完的thin noodle、thick noodle、wide noodle牆角一邊蹲著去了。

✓ 冬粉

聽過Cellophane vermicelli？就是火鍋裡那個冬粉囉。Cellophane是包裝禮物的那種半透明有點反光很薄的玻璃紙，用來形容冬粉的那種半透明感，冬粉在網上常見的翻譯則是Mung bean thin noodles。

✅ 胡蘿蔔 "carrots"

carrot是紅蘿蔔，胡蘿蔔。豌豆和胡蘿蔔 "pea and carrot" 這個拿出來說一下：一個紅的，一個綠的，一般在烹飪時做為點綴，而且常常同時出現，所以引申為形影不離。‹e.g.› 他們之間的關係簡直到了如膠似漆，形影不離的地步"the relationship between them is like pea and carrot."形影不離還有其他幾種說法：

以前我們總是形影不離。

We used to go everything together.

—— 《Chloe》

七歲到九歲，芬妮跟我形影不離。

From the ages of 7 to 9, frannie and I were inseparable.

—— 《Friends 07x11 All The Cheesecakes》

✅ 都有耶 "Check check check."

有有有／搞定／好好好／行行行／勾勾勾。

護照，有。相機，有。旅行支票，有。

Passport, check. Camera, check. Traveler's checks, check.

—— 《Friends 04x23-24 Rosss Wedding》

✅ 咔啦烤雞 "crusted chicken"；咔啦炸雞 "crispy chicken"

咔啦是食材上面加上crumbs（麵包屑，發 ['krʌm]不發 ['krʌmb]）的一種料理方式，吃起來外面會比較脆。美國有些人怕胖，用烤的跟用油炸的不同方式料理有些人很在乎，美國速食店有賣Crusted chicken，亞洲地區烤雞也是有，但是這種加上麵包粉去烤的好像沒在速食店看到，印象中都是炸的Crispy chicken。

→ crumby

形容詞，溫馨提示注意發音，發 ['krʌmɪ] 不發 ['krʌmbɪ]，裏粉或麵包屑油炸，盡是屑粒的，在英國，通常去點炸魚薯條他就會問你魚要做烘的還是炸的 "bake or crumby?"

近音字 **grumpy**

愛生氣的，常形容沒睡夠亂發脾氣的，上床氣，下床氣。

我每次大清早叫醒媽咪她都會發脾氣。
Mommy gets grumpy if I wake her too early.

—— 《*Fringe 01x15*》

✓阿喜上身 "Miss cranky pants've gotten into you"

上身在中文裡有好多意思，以下是各種相對應的英文表達方式：

→ 指附身的那種上身

在這裡阿喜上身的上身是附身的意思，被阿喜附身也可以用 "haunted by Miss cranky pants"，傲驕女神試試這個Feisty goddess（容易興奮激動又或易怒的女神），帶貶意的可以用spoiled bish，bish就是你想的那個字的變音字沒錯 :p中文裡則依地域而有不同說法：如分布於廣大珠江流域以北，奧特曼的妹妹的傲嬌妹。太武山往南以很會張的張三小，或盧不停的盧小小為代表。

開始我以為是因為**Robin**陰魂不散，後來我才發現是因為我自己的問題。

At first, I thought it was haunted by Robin, but now I think it was haunted by me.

—— 《*How I Met Your Mother 07x18*》

它是邪惡的它被附身了。立刻把它脫掉！

It's evil. It's possessed. Take it off right now!

—— 《*Be Wtih You 01x14*》

是不是什麼東西上身了？

What's gotten into you?

—— 《*How I Met Your Mother 08x22*》

你是瑞斯上身了吧。

Reese got in your head.

—— 《*The Newsroom 01x02*》

如果是指光著上身的上身，用topless

我的天！你是說，像是…沒穿衣服？上了每日新聞？

Holy crap! You mean, like... Topless? In The Daily News?

我那時候不是完全光著膀子。他們在暴露的地方貼了馬賽克。

I was not topless. They put a black bar over the exposed area.

—— 《*Everybody Loves Raymond 07x15 The Disciplinarian*》

➔ 指上半身的上身

一邊討論歐巴馬夫人健美的上身。

Talking about Michelle Obama's upper-body workout.

—— 《*New Girl 01x13*》

➔ 那引火上身，惹禍上身的上身呢？

你小心玩火上身。

You're playing a very dangerous game.

—— 《*Modern Family 02x10*》

你多管閒事，現在是惹火上身了。

You meddled, and now they've come for you.

—— 《*Cougar Town 2x11*》

我注意到你們市長惹禍上身了。

I saw that your mayor got himself into a little bit of trouble.

—— 《*Fringe 01x15*》

✔ 那是什麼 "wassat [wɔ•zæt]"

也就是 "what's that?"網上聊天、美國漫畫、口語中常用。怎麼了？
"wassup? / what's up?"

✔ 救人啊幫幫忙 "Yikes"

這個字常用在兩個地方，一個是表達驚嚇、受不了、我的媽呀我的天啊。另一個用在表達食物太難吃難聞，噁心到恐怖，意同Yuck [jʌk]。
近音字 好吃"Yum"。

你現在不能扣籃了。這叫髂腰肌腱炎。通常是說舞者的臀部。

You can't still dunk. It's called iliopsoas tendonitis. It's more commonly known as dancer's hip.

哦，天哪。聽起來太糟了。

Oh, yikes. That sounds bad.

—— 《How I Met Your Mother 04x14 The Possimpible》

噁～他們的房子聞起來一股腳臭味。

Yikes~ Their house smells like feet.

—— 《Everybody Loves Raymond 04x05 The Will》

達人提點

✓ 過敏／會過敏 "allergic / got a sensitivity"

出門在外，多多少少吃不習慣，試著入鄉隨俗，尊重並去享受當地人的美食文化，出外旅遊也不過就那麼幾天，如果跟家裡吃的都一樣，那還有什麼意思是吧。有些度假的小島，看醫生不是那麼方便，還要坐船去另一個島。而領隊導遊不是醫生也不能給藥。自己的身體自己最知道，出門在外備點個人常用藥比較好。海鮮過敏shellfish allergy、shrimp allergy。形容詞是allergic。

我忘了你對生蠔過敏了，嚴重嗎？

I forgot you were allergic to oyster, how bad is it?

—— 《Cougar Town 2x09》

✅ 特別出名的小吃 "specialties"

specialties ['spɛ•ʃəl•tɪz] 招牌菜，團體去的餐廳通常都是簽約，不用點菜。但是也常有客人當日行程結束後，想到附近餐廳包點什麼回旅館打打牙祭。如果客人沒有吃素或一些宗教、健康上的顧慮，點招牌菜倒是挺方便的。

你好有什麼事嗎？戴夫・史令叫的外賣。
Yes, can I help you? Delivery for Dave Shilling.
—— 《*The Bank Job 2008*》

✅ 韓國燒烤

在首爾的時候，客人要吃旅館旁邊的燒烤，餐館老闆帶我們這些歪果仁到一桌剛上菜的客人旁邊，讓大家看著桌上的實品點餐，這群微醺的俊男美女（真的整的太成功好自然！看的我都*Beep*想整 :D）一直熱情地把肉串塞到你手上要你吃吃看他們的美食，反而弄得我的客人不好意思了。我問客人預算多少，他說三萬韓幣，我看每桌上都有烤肋排，想説這應該就是招牌菜了，於是當機立斷跟老闆講三萬塊要有肋排其他看著辦，後來大夥高高興興的帶了香氣四溢疊起來整整三層的烤肋排跟其他兩樣菜回旅館。

該死的快開槍，我當時當機立斷。
Take the bloody shot. I made a judgment call.
—— 《*007 Skyfall 2012*》

我得和Kathryn商量下。　別三心兩意了，當機立斷。
I have to discuss it with Kathryn. Be decisive.
—— 《*Boardwalk Empire 1x09 Belle Femme*》

✅ 散夥飯

有次離開美國前，用剩下的美元請那些曾經在夕陽下一起奔跑的各種屌絲阿宅到從沒去過的高檔餐廳吃散夥飯 "farewell dinner"，忐忑的摸著不知道是混著法語還是義大利文的菜單，一旁站著西裝筆挺側著頭，如同大衛雕像般的dressed-up waiters的望著你，腦中除了空白還是空白，生命中往事的畫面在眼前一幕幕閃過 "My life flash before my eyes"，這菜不知從何點起。就在迴光返照的那一瞬間 "in a stolen moment of dead cat bounce"，本魯莊敬自強的從牙縫中擠出一句 "For the very first time in this lovely place, surprise me." 意思是第一次來貴寶地，你們有什麼像樣的菜色就給林北端上來。接下來就一樣上菜拍照賓主盡歡了，在此跟各位分享這句緊急時候的萬用句 :D

那感覺。忐忑不安，緊張到腸胃不輪轉。

That feeling. The butterflies, the knot in the stomach.

—— 《Secret Diary Of A Call Girl 02x08》

聽我說，如果你不介意的話，我不太想聊天。我現在只想靜靜坐著在腦海裡回顧我的一生。

Listen, if you don't mind, I'm not really up for chatting. I'm just going to sit here quietly and let my life flash before my eyes.

—— 《The Big Bang 05x24》

PART 4

亞洲
風情之浪漫之旅

4.1　促銷High翻天 福建世界文化遺產土樓5日

💬 情境對話

MP3 017

麥可
我們在這裡下車就換坐觀光車，就快到了。
We make a quick change to the golf cart bus here. We're almost there.

Barney
看見了，那個圓圓的房子。
I see it, that circular dwelling.

麥可
各位，客家土樓到了。嗨，小蔣。
Ladies and gentlemen, hakka Tulous. Hi, Chiang.

麥可
接下來由她為我們講解。大家給小蔣拍手歡呼一下！
Next, she will walk us through. Let's hear it for Chiang!

小蔣
謝謝領隊的介紹。
Thank you, Michael for the introduction.

小蔣
歡迎各位的到來！我是小蔣。
Everybody's welcome here! I'm Chiang.

Cobie
她好可愛。
She's cute.

Barney
嘿！妳結婚了嗎？
Hey! Are you married?

才沒有啦…（羞）我今年20歲，在念大三。
Naah... *blush* I'm 20. I'm a junior at university.

巴尼你可以等一下再把電話號碼寫在小紙條上偷偷塞給她。
Barney you can slip her your number later.

小蔣，繼續。
Chiang, keep going.

咳咳。歡迎來到我的家鄉，土樓。
Ahem. Welcome to my hometown, tulous.

目前我們看到的這個牆是由夯土混了石頭構成，防彈的。
This wall is formed by compacting earth which is mixed with stone. It is bullet-proof.

在我左手邊的是外面包鐵皮的大門。
On my left, that's an iron-plate covered main gate.

門上面那大箱子是什麼？
On the top of the gate, what is that tank for?

那個箱子裝滿了沙跟水，設計用來防止敵人火攻。
That is filled with sand and water, designed to prevent the outside gate being set on fire.

如果還擋不住敵人的猛攻呢？
What if it is still unable to survive the enemy's onslaught ['ɑnˌslɔt] ?

小蔣。我會保護你的。我保證。
Chiang. I'll keep you safe. I promise.

在緊急情況下，我們還有條地道可以逃走。
If it's an emergency, we have a tunnel ['tʌ•nl] to escape.

麥可

聽說美國曾一度以為這裡是導彈發射台？
I heard that the US army once mistook the Tulous as missile silos ['saɪlos] ?

小蔣

嗯，是因為這些圓圈狀的屋頂。
Yes, because of those donut-shaped tops.

Cobie

這些屋頂從衛星圖看起來像導彈發射台。
Those tops look like missile silos through satellite ['sæ•təˌlaɪt] footage.

小蔣

你說對了。
You bet.

小蔣

現在請跟我上這建築物的頂樓。
Please follow me to the top level of these earth buildings.

小蔣

在我的右手邊，牆上的洞猜猜是幹什麼的？
On my right, guess what those wall holes are for?

Barney

跟男神一起放風箏的？
Fly a kite with your dreamboat?

小蔣

是射擊孔用來防盜的…
They are gun holes for defensive purposes...

Cobie

嘖嘖，可惜防不了色狼。
Tsk-tsk, too bad they do not work or sex predators.

Barney

嘖嘖，說誰呢？
Cik-cik-cik, who are you calling sex predator?

麥可

好的。謝謝小蔣的導覽，接下來自由活動到5點半。
All right. Thank you Chiang for your service we are free to do as we like until five thirty.

Cobie
我剛隨便逛了一下，麥可你在幹嘛？
I'll just hang around here, what are you doing, Michael?

麥可
你看，小蔣在中庭跳起竹竿舞了。
Look, Chiang is doing a bamboo pole dance on the patio.

Barney
哇哦～她跳的好快！酷斃了！
Wow~ that was fast! Awesome!

Cobie
噢～像是在仙境裡翩翩起舞的蝴蝶。
Aww~ like a butterfly dancing around in fairyland.

✓ 給小蔣拍手歡呼一下 "Let's hear it for Chiang."

Let's hear it有兩種意思，一個是指下面讓我們歡迎誰出場，拍拍手歡呼一下，也可以説make some noise for someone。

讓我們為學校最帥最受歡迎的萬人迷，但GPA只拿了個2分的同學鼓掌。
Let's hear it for our most popular student with a 2.0 grade point average.

—— 《*Everybody Hates Chris 02x22*》

我要聽到你們為我的非洲兄弟歡呼！
Let me hear you make some noise for my African brother!

—— 《*Skins 03x03*》

全都歡呼！

All cheering!

—《Family Guy 09x08 New Kidney In Town》

鼓掌歡呼和尖叫！

Applause, cheering, and whooping!

—《Family Guy 09x09 And I'm Joyce Kinney》

跟老外玩遊戲聊天打字的話，類似以下的這些gesture for party都可以用來帶動氣氛，看完本書就會找到怎麼複製貼上，加油！^^

｡•‿•｡☺☆☆☆☺party groovy whistle☺☆☆☆☺｡•‿•｡｡
ヾ (๑´ڡ`๑) ﾉ♡party animals！
↑↑pump up the volume↑↑｡
↑—partyyypeoplee—↑｡
.+*'`'*+mudda fukka wake up horn+*'`'*+.
Tuuuuuuuuuunes！
Hooo！Hooo！Hooo！

✔ **Let's hear it. 的另外一個意思是說來大家聽聽吧，你說出來我們洗耳恭聽。**

要是有人有更好的建議，說出來我們洗耳恭聽。我沒別的辦法了，大家別害羞。各種建議都可以。

If anyone else has a better suggestion, let's hear it. Because I got nothing! Don't be shy. Any suggestion will do.

—《Friends 05x04 The One Where Phoebe Hates Pbs》

長官，我們認為找到了答案。 說來聽聽。

Sir, we may have found a solution. Let's hear it.

—— 《Stargate 07x09 Avenger 2.0》

✔偷偷塞給 "slip"

這個字有很多用法。做名詞同意書 "permission slip"。

我可以把履歷表塞給伍迪艾倫。

I could slip Woody Allen my resume.

—— 《Friends 04x19 All The Haste》

✔做動詞加上out，"slip out" 指東西的話是滑掉，指人的話是落跑。

我會偷偷塞給他一些錢。 可是要乾淨俐落不著痕跡。

I'll slip him some money. But you've got to be smooth.

—— 《Friends 07x10 The Holiday Armadillo》

你覺得他都已經看到了我們，或者我們還是有機會落跑？

Do you think he saw us, or can we still slip out?

—— 《Friends 08x12 Where Joey Dates Rachel》

我們已經讓瑞秋溜走了，除非有更多資訊否則都是徒勞。

We already let Rachel slip away, there's no point until we have more.

—— 《House Of Cards 02x01》

你也許會想躲進你的性感睡衣裡。

You might want to slip into your negligee ['nɛ•glɪ'ʒe].

—— 《In The Loop 2009》

在我左手邊 "on my left"

也就是on my left side，在我的右邊on my right。我的前方，on my front side，我的後方on my six。

有一些樹在我的左側，距離馬路大概五公尺。
I got trees on my left, maybe five meters off the road.
—— 《Generation Kill 01x05 A Burning Dog》

我真的覺得作為搭檔的**Don**和我關係進展了一大步，這所有的一切都歸功於我左邊的這位女士。
I really think that don and I are hitting our stride as a news team. Well, all credit goes to this lady on my left.
—— 《How I Met Your Mother 05x17 Of Course》

待在我六點鐘的方向，從高處掩護，還有別從後面射到我。
Stay on my six, cover high, and don't shoot me in the back.
—— 《Iron Man 3》

嘖嘖 "tsk-tsk, cik-cik-cik"

嘖嘖，擬聲詞。tsk tsk比較常見，偶而也看過做cik-cik-cik。是個不認同，帶些嘲諷挖苦的擬聲詞。 例如 嘖嘖，他上班又遲到了 "Tsk-tsk, he is late for work again." 又好比某人說，我本來可以當太空人的，然後另一個人好整以暇的回答說 "tsk tsk... And what happened?" 嘖嘖然後呢，這句話並不是真的想知道答案，而是你繼續吹呀的意思。想進一步體會的可以上影片網搜尋Americans，tsk tsk，這是影集《Have I Got News For You》裡的其中一段。

噴噴，珊莎這麼好的為你求一條生路，多可惜就這麼自暴自棄。

Tsk tsk. Sansa pleaded so sweetly for your life, it would be a shame to throw it away.

—— 《*Game Of Thrones 01x09*》

✓ 導覽／講解 "docent service / walk us through"

導覽員docent ['dosənt]，基本是志工性質，也有領薪水的，導覽服務 "docent service / group docent service / interpretive services [ɪn'tə•prə•tɪv]"。

你是得到什麼工作？ 在博物館當導覽員。

What job did you get? Tour guide at the museum.

—— 《*Friends 04x11 Phoebes Uterus*》

他在帶孩子們參觀博物館。

He's showing kids the museum.

—— 《*Bones 04x11*》

✓ 隨便逛了一下 "hang about for a minute"

hang out很常用，這個hang out也有跟朋友一起玩，廝混或坐坐，聊聊的意思。你要我去你房間坐坐嗎？"You want me to hang out in your room?" 我先跟幾個哥們聊聊 "I'll just hang out with the guys."

我們應該一起出去玩。

Yeah. We should all hang out.

—— 《*Modern Family 02x12*》

我們兩個從來都沒有單獨出去玩過。那我們就…那我們就一起吃晚飯，就我們兩個。

You and I never really hang out alone. Well, let's... Let's have dinner together, just the two of us.

—— 《How I Met Your Mother 06x11》

這些人現在已經不能算我真正的朋友了，我不跟她們一起玩了。

Those aren't really my friends anymore. I don't hang out with them.

—— 《Parks And R 01x04 Boys Club》

一起玩／鬧著玩 "fooling around, goofing around"

fooling around帶有男女間的那種曖昧的，goofing around瞎混攪和不認真的。

反正你跟我只是玩玩而已，所以我想，我也可以跟他玩玩。

Well, you and I are just goofing around. I thought, why not just goof around with him?

—— 《Friends 09x10 Christmas In Tulsa》

逛一圈／逛一下／到處看看 "walk around / go look around / kick around"

我沒買東西。我們只是逛了一會。

I didn't buy anything. We just walked around for awhile.

—— 《Everybody Loves Raymond 04x22 Bad Moon Rising》

你用一個小時就可以逛一圈。

You could walk around it in an hour.

—— 《007 Skyfall 2012 720P Bluray x264-Daa》

我們再多逛一下。

We're just gonna go look around a little more.

—— 《*Cougar Town 1x02*》

 達人提點

✔ improvise，freestyle

沒有劇本的即席創作，即興表演。導遊人員如果只是把當地的風景書看完，不管客人是藍領白領老人小孩都照本宣科的讀一次，這樣不但客人有如聽錄音般的枯燥感，自己也容易對這份工作失去熱情，試試就算同樣的景點也多準備幾個口味不同的梗或段子，隨團性靈活運用。深入淺出的當作是個脫口秀講解，適度的跟客人互動。注意，客人張大眼睛仔細聽還邊點頭，並不一定表示他們喜歡導遊不當的講解，有時是在盤算到了購物站後要如何尿遁XD，隨著經驗逐漸修正，多練習幾次拿捏分寸。頭痛就醫頭，腳痛就醫腳，並想想腳累是不是鞋墊太滑引起的，頭痛是不是睡覺時對著冷氣出風口引起的，試著去思考問題背後的原因。

不好意思，我沒有照劇本來。

I'm sorry I'm going off script.

—— 《*Modern Family 02x08*》

我並不介意你臨場自由發揮。

I don't mind that you improvised ['ɪm•prə•vaɪzd].

—— 《*House Of Cards 01x06*》

你要照按規矩辦事嗎？ 不，我要自由發揮。

Do you want to nail the line? No, I'll freestyle it.

—— 《*In The Loop 2009*》

✔leeway

相對於上面提到的自由揮灑，另一個近似但又不太一樣的字是leeway，指的是一定範圍內的彈性，字面上的解釋是風壓差，風壓角，偏航，引申為可允許的誤差，稍微有點偏了再繞回來只要能到達目的地也沒關係，迴旋餘地，這種感覺。

如果能多給我點自由發揮的空間就更好了。
It'd be great if I had a little leeway.

—— 《House Of Cards 02x10》

那你上司知道你多管閒事了。是的，他給了我自己一點自由揮灑的餘地。

Your boss knows you've drifted outside the circle? Yeah, he's giving me a little leeway.

—— 《Perception 01x06》

4.2 華麗假期 長灘島風帆夕陽絕色、 絕愛、絕對浪漫

💬 情境對話

MP3 018

接下來我們去坐風帆。
Now we're going sailing.

麥可

看夕陽。
To watch the sunset.

麥可

請把救生衣穿起來。
Put on your life jackets, please.

麥可

我看起來怎麼樣？嗯…
How do I look? Hmm...

Cobie

我再也不穿救生衣了，看起來好胖。
I will never wear a life vest. It makes me look fat.

Cobie

很配妳陽光的膚色，不是嗎？
It suits your light tan complexion [kəm'plɛk•ʃən] , don't you think?

麥可

那我呢？
How about me?

Barney

你像外勞。
You look foreign.

Cobie

好了，別說了。歡迎登船。
Hey, knock it off. Welcome on board.

太棒了。我要拍些照。
This is amazing. I wanna snap some shots.

當浪打來的時候，船頭激起的水花會濺濕相機.
When the bow spray comes over, the water might damage the camera .

準備好防水袋喔。
Get your waterproof pouch ready okay.

嗯。
Okay.

你無論如何都不能錯過長灘的風帆。
You wouldn't miss the parasailing for the world.

在原始的帆船上整個人放空。
While relaxing on this traditional sailing boat.

當這船隨著海浪起伏。
As the boat undulates ['ʌndʒə,let] in rhythm with wave.

用野生的方式來航向如畫般的夕陽。
Experience the traditional way of sailing off into the incredible sunset.

麥可，你注意過嗎？
Michael, have you ever noticed?

這夕陽看起來份外美麗，在你和你心上的那個人分享的時候。
The sunset looks more beautiful, when you share it with someone you care about?

麥可

完全同意。
I'll say.

Barney

你知道嗎？
You know what.

Barney

你比黃澄澄的夕陽還可愛。
You're lovelier than the golden sunset.

麥可

哈哈，別搞基了。
HaHa, no bromance pal.

Barney

別理我。啊對了麥可，你有女朋友嗎？
Ignore me. Uh by the way Michael, you got a girlfriend?

麥可

我的女朋友迷了路，到現在還找不到我。
My girlfriend made a wrong turn. She just doesn't know where to find me.

Barney

哈哈哈。
HAHAHA.

Cobie

人類已經無法阻止他了。
There's no stopping this guy, he's not human.

Cobie

天色晚了。
It's getting late.

Barney

嗯啊，是有點晚了。
Uh-huh, it's pretty kinda late.

場景：蔻比一時興起對著晚霞哼起歌來。
Cobie hummin' to the afterglow on the spur of the moment.
（想聽這首歌嗎親？搜尋Birds Ana Egge ^^）

Cobie
夕陽西下
And the sun sets

Cobie
鳥兒撲起
All the birds rise

Cobie
迎面飛來
Up to me

Cobie
巴尼,我看起來怎樣?
Barney, how do I look?

Barney
我該怎麼回答?
What do I tell her?

麥可
跟她說,她看起來讓人很想親一口。
(對巴尼耳語/Whispering in his ear)
Tell her, she looks like someone who's about to get kissed.

Barney
嗯…懂了。(擊掌)
Well... Get it. *fistbump*

Cobie
所以呢巴尼,我看起來怎樣?
So Barney, how do I look?

Barney
咳咳…你不肥!
Ahem... NOT FAT!

☆ 單詞與句型

膚色／膚質 "complexion"

柔膚水 "complexion mist / facial spray"。把燕麥跟牛糞打勻用來敷臉很好，至少年輕十歲！"a nice mixture of oatmeal mud and cow shit is very good for the complexion, takes 10 years off at least!"（此為節目效果，請勿在家嚐試）

你是不是抹口紅了 這叫「媚惑紅」？很配我白皙的膚色，你不覺得嗎？
Are you wearing lipstick? It's called "Ravish Me Red." It suits my porcelain complexion, don't you think?

—— 《American Horror Story 02x03》

潤膚露⋯哇，好東西。我知道你皮膚好的秘訣了。
The moist face lotion... Wow, this is great stuff. Now I know the secret to your great complexion.

—— 《How I Met Your Mother 02x16 Stuff》

所以 M-A-6-L-T 是描述：男性。亞裔，6英尺高，膚色淺。
So the M-A-6-L-T is a description: male. Asian, six feet tall, light complexion.

—— 《Hawaii Five O 01x13》

無論如何都 "for the world"

錯過全世界我也不會錯過這個。
I wouldn't miss this for the world.

—— 《Everybody Loves Raymond 07x21 The Shower》

因為我得到了一件我千金也不換的東西，那就是我們的友情。

Because it led me to something that I wouldn't trade for the world. It led to you being my friend.

—— 《How I Met Your Mother 08x11-12》

我們的要求並不過分。

We're not asking for the world.

—— 《House Of Cards 01x05》

✓完全同意 "I'll say."

深有同感，我也會這樣說，我也正想這麼說，換作我說也一樣。

那太對了。

That's so true.

—— 《How I Met Your Mother 03x03 Third Wheel》

幹這行靠本事不靠運氣。　說得沒錯。

We make our own luck. True enough.

—— 《Boardwalk Empire 1x01 Boardwalk Empire》

可不是嗎？（嘆）

You can say that again. *sighs*

—— 《Family Guy 09x14 Tiegs For Two》

我猜又是可惡的郵局搞砸的。就是！

I guess there was some screw-up at the damn post office. Tell me about it!

—— 《Friends 07x20 Rachel's Big Kiss》

✅ 搞基 "bromance"

被惡搞成基情，拆開給你看Brother Romance。指袍澤之情用brotherhood。

相關的還有 "Romance or No-mance?" 這句有累覺不愛的Fu（累了感覺不會再愛了）。

我恨死情人節了，不只是商業化的炒作，還有搞得對方也就這一天應付你。

I hate the idea of valentines day! Not just for the commercialism, for the whole idea of "I'll treat you special this ONE DAY."

既然講到累覺不愛，順便記一下十動然拒（十分動心但是斷然拒絕），"I cry, but decline."

✅ 別理我 "ignore me"

當我沒說，常見的有forget it、forget about it、never mind。還有以下的例子：

算了，當我沒說。

Actually, do you know what? Ignore me.

—— 《Sherlock 01x01》

剛才我抱怨這傢伙無聊，當我沒說。

What I said about our guy being boring, I take it back.

—— 《Person Of Interest 01x03》

你是對的你是對的我明白了當我沒說。

You're right, you're right. I got it. Forget I said anything.

—— 《How I Met Your Mother 07x22》

在某些情況下fair enough，也有表達我懶的說了，當我沒說的意思。

我去幫別人忙是錯的？幫兩個小偷？當我沒說。

I was wrong for trying to help two people? Two burglars? Fair enough.

—— 《Modern Family 02x08》

放空 "relaxing"

伸伸懶腰腦袋放空。"foot loose and fancy free"。有句話說，頻頻回頭的人走不了遠路，永不回頭的人容易走錯路。偶而放慢腳步，回頭看看自己在哪裡，就像畫要有留白，樂章要有停頓。慢活"The Slow Movement"讓人活得比較像個人，為自己而活。

而不是活在別人眼光裡的奴隸。例如 他是一個汲汲營營勾心鬥角的小人 "He is everything vile." 把名韁利鎖 "handcuffs and fetters of fame and fortune" 往自己頭上套的喘不過氣。

我就讓我的大腦完全…呼算了吧！放空。

I just keep my brain totally... Pfft! Empty.

—— 《Cougar Town 2x11》

→ 發呆 "stare [stɛr] into space / staring off"

你只是在發呆。

You're just staring into space.

—— 《Friends 6x03 Rosss Denial》

我只是神情茫然的發呆。

I'm just staring vacantly into space.

—— 《In The Loop 2009 》

有一次她發現我在發呆。

Oh, one time she caught me staring off.

—— 《Modern Family 2x06》

晚霞 "afterglow"

晚霞，回味afterglow ['æf•tə•glo]。

我們沉浸在勝利的餘味之中。

We basked in the afterglow of victory.

他沉浸在愛情的甜蜜回憶之中。

He was basking in the afterglow of love.

擊掌 "fistbump"

擊拳，跟high five一樣的意思。

我們不許擊拳，擊掌。

No fist bumping. No high fives.

—— 《2 Broke Girls 02x04》

你不跟我擊掌，我的手就不放下。

I'm not dropping my hand until you five it.

―― 《*Cougar Town 2x1x22*》

除了high five，還有low five，也是擊掌，就是手不舉高，西方人很活潑，這類花里胡哨的肢體語言可老多了。有人說擊拳比握手衛生多了，我也覺得。

Barney：擊掌！

　　　　High five!

TED：兄弟，我們可是在守靈。

　　　Dude, we're at a wake.

Barney：對不起，那嚴肅的低調擊掌一下吧。

　　　　Sorry. Solemn ['sɑləm] low five.

　　　　―― 《*How I Met Your Mother 02x14 Monday Night Football*》

 **達人提點**

✅ 坐風帆 "go sailing"

坐風帆看夕陽，金速配 "a perfect match"，但是我也有遇過坐風帆看太陽中午12點曬人乾的。

➜ 拖鞋還有分？不是隨便帶就好？

水上活動不管是風帆，浮潛，拖曳傘 "Beach Parasailing" 或就是玩水，拖鞋記得要穿不吸水的 "no spongy"，有個某牌的麂皮瑜珈墊人字拖就不太適合泡水裡，出海的話可以帶點水果去，看著碧海藍天心情本來就好，泡泡水玩玩水拍拍照流流汗，回到船上，大太陽曬一曬口渴了，正好拿出水果來，海水潑上來等於加點免費甘草鹽，怎麼吃都好吃よ～よ～

我有沒有告訴你我去浮潛啦？

Did I tell you I went snorkelling?

—— 《Secret Diary Of A Call Girl 04x01》

你只有想在我的熱水池玩水時才來找我。

（一個無事不登三寶殿的朋友）

You only come around when you want to play pool in my hot tub.

—— 《Childish Gambino The Worst Guys》

✔ 注意小細節

輕鬆度假的地方，適度的跟客人保持距離，讓他們玩他們的。反正就那麼大個島，不拉車不換旅館不趕景點購物站，頂多坐坐船Island hopping。晚餐若是海邊BBQ，大家都是擠在同一個時間吃飯，人多了，廚師有時急著上菜，客人吃1個生蠔可能沒事，要是吃10個（我遇過吃20幾個的），就不知道腸胃hold不hold的住了，記得交代一下廚師當生蠔開了的時候，多烤個30秒再上菜 "When the grill pops the shell open, just hold on for another 30 seconds, then serve." 這種簡單英文當地人都聽得懂，就算導遊或地陪不在，也不用擔心溝通會有問題。

✅ 領隊外宿

如果領隊外宿，那晚上就沒什麼事，長灘民宿一般沒有熱水，天氣挺好的不會冷，真的洗不慣冷水的，回房早點洗或一桶冷水從頭上澆下去接著就比較不冷了。

4.3 限量版、直飛6日 無憂無慮菲律賓長灘、夜店

情境對話

 MP3 019

Barney

聽說有家夜店叫做摳摳夢哥濕。
I heard there is a club called Cocomangas Shooter Bar.

Cobie

重點是什麼？怎麼個好玩法？
What's the point? How is that fun?

Barney

可好玩了，我們叫15杯酒，喝完可以得到一件個性T恤。
Heaps of fun, we order the 15 Shots, and the winner gets a Logo T-shirt.

Barney

這T恤上面印有…
A T-shirt that says...

Barney

喝完15杯仍然屹立不倒的人！
Still standing after fifteen!

Cobie

那有什麼？真是幼稚你們男生。
What's the big deal? Boys never grow up.

Barney

牆上還有個刻有你名字的小銅牌。
A little brass plaque with your name on the wall.

Cobie

我又喝不多。
I don't drink much.

Barney

麥可去嗎？我們大家一起去見識見識嘛。
Michael, you in? We've all set out to prove something.

麥可

我得對明天的行程，我叫導遊陪你們去。
Got to check the plan for tomorrow, I will send the tour guide there.

Cobie

（噗哧）6天都就在這島上，對個屁。
Chuckle Six days on an island, check my ass.

Cobie

你去我就去。
I'll go if you'll go with me.

Barney

對啊，導遊跟我們去你跟誰對行程。
Yeah, who can check the plan, if the tour guide goes with us.

Barney

一起去啦，別掃興。
We're all going, don't be a party pooper.

麥可

明早自由活動，下午集合後開飯。
Tomorrow morning is free. Buffet for lunch, followed by the afternoon meeting.

Cobie

大家歡呼～～
Everybody says YAAAAAAAYYY~~

Barney

整裝！出發！
Suit up! Giddy ['gɪdɪ] up!

Barney

我到了，終於到了！乾杯！
I made it. I made it! Cheers!

Cobie

你們想跳舞嗎？我要去跳舞，尖叫ing～～
You want to dance? I'm going to dance. Wooooooot~ ~

Barney

這是不是假酒？
Does this have alcohol in it?

麥可

什麼？不會吧，為什麼！？
What? No way, why!?

Barney

喝不醉耶我一點事兒都沒，奇怪。ㄎㄎㄎㄎ～
I don't feel a thing, weird. Hahahaha~

Cobie

嘖嘖嘖…你就繼續吹吧。讓我們繼續看下去。
Tsk tsk tsk... You keep bluffing. We'll see.

Cobie

有誰能告訴我！我的白馬王子在哪裡？！（狂吹口哨）
Someone tell me, where is MY SHINING ARMOR?!
Insane whistling

Barney

乾杯了，我的T恤呢？！
Buttom's up, where is my T-Shirt?!

Barney

我現在要換裝變身了，你們不准看我的小肚腩！
I'll put on the T-Shirt right now right here, DON'T YOU
stare at my muffin-top!

Cobie

好醜的T恤…（咯咯笑）
What an ugly T-Shirt... *Giggle*

Cobie

麥可！舉杯來點精彩的敬酒詞！
Michael! Raise your glasses and make a nice toast!

麥可

噹噹噹（敲杯子）～本魯謹祝各位貴賓，新年快樂，萬事如意。
Clang clang clang~ I would like to raise a toast to our
guests, Happy New Year and I wish you all the best and
every success.

Cobie
切，打這種官腔。
Crap, that is management talk.

Barney
也許我喝多了。
I may have had too much to drink.

Barney
我這個黑暗街的酒家男醉的風中各種凌亂了。
This party animal is three sheets to the wind now.

Cobie
我是沒醉…我只是…如果我說錯話…
I'm fine. I'm just... If I say anything weird...

麥可
玩夠了，回頭飯店見吧。
That's enough of that. I'll meet you back at the hotel.

謎之音))) 別走開廣告之後馬上回來！Stay where you are and we'll be right back after this short commercial break!

Waitress
不好意思讓一讓，上酒。
Excuse me, here you go.

Barney
又來15杯？借問一下，現在是什麼情形？
Another 15 shots? EXCUSE ME, WHAT IS THIS ALL ABOUT?

Cobie
我點的，人家就要那個T恤嘛…
I ordered another round, Cobie really want that T-Shirt...

☆ 單詞與句型

✓ 這聽起來好像 "That sounds like..."

是啊，聽起來好像也對。

Yeah, that sounds about right.

—— 《*Friends 09x12 Phoebes Rats*》

我聽起來好像也許…。也許你不太爽。

Sounds to me like maybe... Maybe you're not so okay with it.

—— 《*Everybody Loves Raymond 06x09 Older Women*》

✓ 人家就要那個T恤嘛 "Cobie really want that T-Shirt"

不說I或me，直接唸出自己的名字就有中文那個「人家」的味道哦，名字代表的是自己，I、me，後面如果接助動詞，用don't不用doesn't，接動詞的話，如want不加s。

✓ 假酒 "adulterated wine"

adulterated wine，adulterate [əˈdʌl•tə•ret] 是攙雜，攙假的意思。反義字unadulterated就是不參雜任何雜質的。

這件事會一直永遠是純潔的，不參雜任何雜質的，美好的。

It will always, always be pure, unadulterated, awesome.

—— 《*How I Met Your Mother 01x13 Drumroll Please*》

✓ 女服務員 "waitress"

各種服務員，廁所門口收小費的the bathroom attendant，女店員可以說shopgirl，房務員叫chambermaid，餐館咖啡廳點菜端菜的waitress。注意busboy可不是開巴士的，而是在餐館裡打雜，一般是推著餐車收吃剩的碗盤的。

以上提到的這些名詞，一般都是她們稱呼自己或你我之間聊到該女服務員的時候說，如果是當著她的面，當然也有人是直接這麼叫。比較入流的方式是稱呼Miss，或者不稱呼，要什麼就Can we have，然後你要點什麼，比如說Coffee，後面加個Please，這樣你除了得到一杯咖啡之外，也許還能得到一個微笑。

能拿點餐巾紙嗎。

Oh, uh, can we have some napkins, please?

—— 《Modern Family 02x13》

字典上的翻譯，現實生活中其稱呼有時並不合適

Maid要翻譯成清潔工沒什麼不對，查字典上面寫的是，女傭女僕，但是現實生活是有誰會這樣講啦，都馬說打掃阿姨，或名字後面加個姨，姊或嫂。英文裡也是一樣，就算不當她的面，也很少聽到講什麼傭人Maid的，來家裡幫忙打掃衛生的就叫Clean lady。也可以說管家domestic helper。

小姐，我要點餐。

Miss, I'm ready to order.

—— 《2 Broke Girls 02x01》

✓ 點早餐

這是一段連珠炮似的問你要點怎樣的雞蛋。「謎之音」媽媽終於不用擔心我不會點雞蛋了 ^^Y。

你要一個兩個還是三個雞蛋？

Would you like one or two or three?

只要蛋白還是跟蛋黃一起？

Whites only with yolks?

炒散蛋？水煮荷包蛋？還是煎一面？煎兩面蛋黃全熟，或煎兩面蛋黃不熟？

Scrambled? Poached? Or fried-sunny-side up, over, or over-easy?

然後你可以學電影 As Good as It Gets 中，Jack Nicholson 對飾演女服務生的Helen · Hunt說：

兩個香腸。

Two sausages.

六個培根，薯條。

Six bacon strips, fries.

三個雞蛋，煎兩面蛋黃不熟，還有咖啡。

Three eggs over easy and coffee.

✔醉的風中各種凌亂 "three sheets to the wind"

醉的風中各種凌亂了，醉得跌跌撞撞了，形容酒醉可約略分以下四個表達方式：

1. 起駕。tipsy微醺，酒精發生作用了，有點嗨，話開始變多了。

2. 上轎。搖搖晃晃，走路不穩 "three sheets to the wind"，帆船上的三片帆都沒綁好，這船就會隨著失控的帆被風吹的東倒西歪，引申用來形容喝醉酒的樣子。如果你覺得三片還不過癮，也可以再加一片變四片，來一句 "Barney was four sheets to the wind."

3.八卡。爛醉，神志不清了 "wasted / hammered / plastered"。我昨晚喝得馬西馬西 "I was so hammered last night."

4.孔鏘。醉倒，醉得不省人事了 "passed out"，醉倒在餐桌上 "passed out on the kitchen table"。

5.宿醉 "hang over"。

✅ 官腔 "management talking"

打官腔／說官話／說套話／沒誠意的制式發言。

別再搞那些官腔了，明白嗎？
Back off the rhetoric, understand?
—— 《Person Of Interest 01x13》

你從那學來這種官僚的屁話？
Where do you get this bureaucratic [bjʊ•rə'kræ•tɪk] bull?
—— 《Stargate 01x21 Politics-Part 1》

近音字 客氣話／客套話／場面話 "social nonsense / pleasantry ['plɛ•zən•trɪ]"

好吃極了，我可不是說客套話。
It is gorgeous, and I'm not just saying that.
—— 《Chinese Food Made Easy 01x05》

他們互相說了一些客套話。然後…閒聊，閒聊，還是閒聊。
They exchanged pleasantries. And... Small talk, small talk, small talk.
—— 《Hawaii Five O 02x06》

科諾・卡拉卡瓦。來自50特警隊。歡迎。史蒂夫對你的評價很高呢。

Kono Kalakaua. Hawaii Five-O. Welcome. Steve speaks very highly of you.

嗯，好了，客套話夠了。

Yeah, all right, enough with the pleasantries.

—《*Hawaii Five O 02x21*》

✔ 白馬王子／高富帥／男神 "Shining armor / Mr. Right / Prince Charming"

你和那男神進展如何？

How'd it go with Fancyman?

—《*New Girl 01x18*》

這就是典型的你，總是奔向你的白馬王子。

It's typical Laurel. Always running to a white knight.

—《*Arrow 01x08 Vendetta*》

瑞秋，準備好了沒，你的白馬王子來了。

Rachel, ready or not, here comes your knight in shining.

—《*Friends 02x14 The Prom Video*》

姐一直期待著跟個富二代生孩子。萬萬沒想到下場會是跟著這個衰尾道人？！

I was expecting some rich dude to knock me up. How did I end up with this sorry bunch?!

—《問世間情為何物之千金難買早知道》

女神可以用 "goddess / dream gril / unicorn"，她是我遙不可及的女神 "She is my unicorn"，有那種too good to be true的感覺。她太美太夢幻 不像是真的 "Unreal"。

哥一直期待著能遇到位性感女神，結果來了個女神經病。
I was hoping I'd run into a lady sexy, and a lady psycho shows up.

—— 《問世間情為何物之萬般無奈想不到》

兩位都是性感女神。
Both of you are sex goddesses.

—— 《Girls 01x01》

嗨，我朝思暮想的夢中情人。
Hey, girl of my dreams.

—— 《Inf-Mmarch》

達人提點

✓ 別掃興 "don't be a party pooper"

poop是便便的意思，pooper是便便的人，在party上poop，這派對還用開 嗎？所以party pooper跟joy killer一樣，都是指掃興的人。當然沒人想當 掃興鬼，但是這個分寸拿捏…比如遇到酒國英雄型的客人，如果能事先 推薦他們包燒烤或下酒菜回旅館吃喝，這樣就隨他們愛怎麼喝了。如果 到外面去玩，要看團性，有些就嗯…適可而止。

✔關於酒

先別說你的自制力靠不靠譜，就算你能喝 "even you can handle your Scotch"，你哪知道這些認識不到2天的客人的酒量？酒品呢？會不會盧？當然專門帶酒莊品酒會的領隊就不在此列了。敢進廚房就不怕熱，覺悟吧 :p。

→ 蘇格蘭威士忌 **"Scotch Whisky"** 或直接簡稱Scotch。

我酒量不好可以這麼說 **"I don't drink well."** 他酒量不好或酒品不好都可以說 **"He couldn't handle his booze."**

→ 她很愛盧小小 **"She always went nuts over nothing."**

謎之音))) 別這句盧小小翻譯的這麼機智有莫有？討拍拍求表揚 **"May I have a pat on the back?"** :D

→ 酒莊 **"wineries"**。品酒會 **"wine-tasting party"**

→ 覺悟吧 **"Suck it / Suck it up / Get over it."**。

指很能喝，酒量好，牛飲，或酗酒。要看上下文，不一定是貶意。
Drinking like a fish.

—— 《Shameless Us 02X11》

沒真的醉過。我酒量好。
Never been really drunk. I have a monster tolerance.

—— 《Cougar Town 1X15》

4.4 品味五星峇里
頂級奢華、浪漫晚宴

情境對話

 MP3 020

Henry

晚餐吃這家餐廳嗎？
Are we gonna have a dinner at this restaurant?

麥可

對，但是我們不在餐廳裡吃。
Yep, but we won't have it inside.

Henry

小朋友！別亂跑！
Boys! Don't rush around!

麥可

乖喔。這邊走然後右轉，你可以在那裡洗手。
Be nice. This way then turn left, you can wash your hands there.

Henry

小朋友你洗好了嗎？過來跟麥可一起走。
Little dude you all done? Come walking with Michael.

麥可

出這個門走樓梯下去。
Go through this door and go downstairs.

麥可

我們在沙灘上有個浪漫的晚宴。
We'll have a romantic dinner on the beach.

Henry

轉過臉迎著風吹，好舒服。
I turn my face to wherever the wind blows. I like that.

Henry
我居然好久沒試過這樣了。
I can't believe I haven't done this for such a long time.

麥可
小確幸嗯？
Pretty little things we can count on huh?

麥可
請大家試著找找看有個牌子上寫著我的名字的，那就是我們的座位。
Guys please find a reservation card with my name on it. That's our table.

Henry
哇！魚蝦蟹！應有盡有！
Wow! Fish, shrimp, crab, you name it!

Henry
啊…怎麼沒有青菜？
Well… Where's the greens?

麥可
等一下就會上青菜。
They'll serve the greens later.

麥可
啊噢。
Oops.

Henry
怎麼了？
Sup?

麥可
蟹螯沒拍碎，我叫他們拿蟹鉗夾來。
The claws aren't cracked, I'll ask them to bring the lobster cracker.

麥可
那邊有海灘樂團穿著色彩繽紛的傳統服裝。
A beach band in a colorful traditional dress over there.

麥可
他們會過來穿梭於各桌間演奏吉他和手鼓。
They'll come by strolling around tables and play guitar and bongos.

Henry

我不知道該給多少小費？
I don't know what to tip?

麥可

一塊美金或一萬印尼幣可以了。
One US Dollar or 10,000 Rupiah will be fine.

麥可

好，開吃了！
Okay, eat up!

Henry

這個披薩怎麼上面都沒有餡料？開什麼玩笑。
Why are there no toppings on pizza? You must be kidding.

麥可

真的嗎？讓我看看。
Really? Let me see that.

麥可

你拿反了，盒子要從這面開。
You put it upside down, open the pizza box from this side.

Henry

呃…
Err…

Henry

這邊阿多仔很多喔。
A lot of Caucasians here.

麥可

對啊，澳洲的達爾文市飛這裡一個半小時就到了。
Yeah, Darwin, Australia is only one and a half hours away by plane.

Henry

血紅夕陽下的沙灘，燭光搖曳的晚餐，輕快曼妙的吉他跟手鼓。
Sanguine sunset at beach, dinner by flickering candle light, a sprightly guitar and bongos.

我沒想到會這麼爽！
I didn't expect this!

領隊來啦！過來跟我們一起吃啦！
Michael come on! Join us!

導遊在等我。甘溫拿，各位慢用。
The tour guide needs me. Thanks a lot. You guys enjoy ^^.

☆ 單詞與句型

✅ 在沙灘上 "on the beach"

waterfront是水邊沿岸的地方，比如說水岸邊的平台。

✅ 風吹 "wind blows"

刮起一道靈風，a spiritual wind blows ['spɪ•rɪ•tʃʊəl]

有人剛才感到一陣陰風嘛？
Did someone just feel a cold breeze?

—— 《*The Big Bang 02x08*》

→ 用來形容困難與阻力

無論遇到怎樣的逆境，我也會逆風高飛。
"No matter how hard the wind blows against me, I'll make the best of a bad situation."

➔ 用來搞文藝

我只想漫無目的的隨風飄啊蕩啊～（其實通常也也不過就是飄到隔壁的巷子）

I'm just gonna drive wherever the wind blows me~ "Which is usually into the next lane."

—— 《Modern Family 01x21》

➔ 形容風吹草動

我會像獵犬一樣追你到天涯海角，每當你聽到任何風吹草動的時候，你就知道我找上門了。

I'm gonna hunt you down like a dog, every time you hear the wind blows, you believe I'm coming.

—— 《Hawaii Five O 01x21》

➔ 風吹也可以用 breeze

你聞出什麼味道來了。像是夏日的和風。

What does he smell like? A summer breeze.

—— 《Everybody Loves Raymond 01X10 Turkey Or Fish》

突然吹來一陣秋風把一個女生的裙子吹了起來。

This lovely fall breeze came and blew this chick's skirt up.

—— 《Friends 05x08 The One With The Thanksgiving Flashbacks》

學了這麼多用法，聽一首跟風有關的歌獎勵自己一下，搜尋 "Stina Nordenstam Fireworks" ^^ 。

♪The train just stopped（列車剛停下了腳步）

But you gave me no chance♪（但你一點機會都不給我）

♪I turn my face to from wherever the wind blows（我把臉迎向那八方撲面而來的風）

Is it worth so much to try♪（真的值得如此努力追你嗎）

✅ 小確幸 "pretty little things"

小確幸，pretty little things，後面加上個we can count on更有Fu。小確幸讓人在人生中常有機會停下腳步快樂一下，而不是貪婪無度如強迫症 "OCD / Obsessive Compulsive Disorder" 般的追求利潤ㄟ（ ˇ ＿ ˇ ）ㄏ

強迫症的人會在生活中不斷重複某種模式，以逃避精神上的恐慌。

People with OCD repeat patterns in their lives in order, to stave off psychological panic.

—— 《Bones 04x05》

✅ 我不知道該給多少小費 "I don't know what to tip."

很多人是靠這個吃飯的，這算一種美國文化。小費有時不只是錢的問題了，而是一種禮貌。給得少的或沒給的也會被戴上小氣，佔人便宜以及沒禮貌的帽子。又或超市買了大包小包回家，有些鄰居的小孩子幫忙你拿進屋，你說聲謝謝關上門他也不會跟你要小費，但是給一塊美金小孩子歡天喜地的跑去買糖吃了，很可愛不是嗎？

我是靠小費吃飯的。

I make my living on tips.

—— 《New Girl 01x10》

今天小費多嗎？

Good tips today?

—— 《Person Of Interest 01x03》

怎麼回事小費才20趴，我做錯事了嗎？　20趴很大方了（在餐館小費一般是給餐費的一成到兩成）

Hey, so, what's with the 20 percent tip? Did I do something wrong? 20 percent is a pretty generous tip.

—— 《Friends 06x17 Unagi》

→ 沒小費

我不會給你小費的，老哥。

I'm not tipping you, brother.

—— 《Everybody Loves Raymond 03x01 The Invasion》

→ 給小費

謝了，親。這給你的。

Thanks, sweetie. Here's for you.

—— 《Boardwalk Empire 1x06 Family Limitation》

別忘給小費。

Don't forget to tip.

—— 《Person Of Interest 01x16》

給你的女侍點小費。

Yep, tip your waitresses.

—— 《The Big Bang 01x09》

我來付小費。

I'll get the tip.

—— 《*Hustle 01x01 The Con Is Onmafriki*》

→ **bad tips** "很少的小費"

我要把這點少得可憐的小費拍下來，然後放到圖片分享網。以前收到稀稀落落的零錢會難過，但是現在我可以跟陌生人分享一下。

I wanna take a picture of this bad tip and put it on Instagram. Getting loose change used to be so depressing, but now I can share it with strangers.

—— 《*2 Broke Girls 02x02*》

小費別給少了，我們都知道你現在是大戶了。

Don't cheap out on the tip, we all know you're loaded now.

—— 《*The Big Bang 05x04*》

她還奇怪為什麼她的小費總是那麼少。

And she wonders why she's constantly undertipped.

—— 《*The Big Bang 03x07*》

→ 多給點小費／多給點打賞 "**tip them good / well**"

多給她點小費，她真是個美女，這裡這個。

Tip her good. She's a real beauty, this one.

—— 《*Boardwalk Empire 1x06 Family Limitation*》

這是服務員溫蒂，多打賞她點。

It's Wendy the waitress. Tip her well.

—— 《How I Met Your Mother 01x21 Milk》

我總是給很多的小費。

I always leave a big tip.

—— 《Everybody Loves Raymond 04x14 Prodigal Son》

找個話題聊聊，你會拿到更多小費。

Make chitchat. You'll get more tips.

—— 《Bobs Burgers 01x06》

✔ 吝嗇的顧客 "horrible tipper"；慷慨的顧客 "a great tipper"

他們小費都給得很吝嗇。

They were both horrible tippers.

—— 《Friends 07x13 Where Rosita Dies》

比如Mitchell Rothman。他是我較為國際化的客戶之一，並且就像所有的美國人一樣…小費給的大方。

Take Mitchell Rothman. He's one of my more international clients, and like all Americans...a great tipper.

—— 《Secret Diary Of A Call Girl 01x08》

→ 給太多

我小費給的太多了。

I tip way too much. Way too much.

—— 《Friends 03x07 The Race Car Bed》

→ **tip**除了小費外，也是線索，提示，忠告

你要的東西在這裡，爸，小費給多少都行。 那就給你一個忠告。
Here you go, dad. Feel free to tip. Here's one for you.
—— 《*Hannah Montana Oops I Meddled Again-Hibocbii*》

達人提點

✔ 盛情難卻 "hard to turn down"

因為我們有時候會巡桌盯餐點，看菜有沒有問題，所以常會有客氣的客人熱情邀約坐下來一起吃，而餐點是算好的，一人一份不會多，那如果是自助餐沒有限量呢？就算這種情況也盡量避免，不要造成氣氛變成好像你跟某些客人特別好，無意中間接造成其他團員有受到冷落的感覺。

我不想讓她覺得備受冷落。
I don't want her to feel left out.
—— 《*2 Broke Girls 02x22*》

無論什麼活動我總是被冷落…
I was always left out of everything...
—— 《*Friends 10x12 Phoebe's Wedding*》

✔ 眼觀四面耳聽八方 "to mind your surroundings."

有心想當through guide的，除了過人的體力跟敏銳的觀察之外，多了解不同國家不同導遊的棱棱角角也很重要。當然在旅程中不要去干涉導遊的操作，這點很忌諱，但這並不意味著上車客人睡覺你也睡覺，客人吃

飯看風景你也吃飯看風景，不說話也要注意細節，比如購物做不好、導遊抱怨怎麼處理？或者換旅館上車時行李總共幾件，導遊有算過嗎？當然前提是你已經有算過。

別裝傻，戈登。我最恨別人裝傻。這是我最忌諱的一點，可以嗎？
Don't play dumb, gordon. I hate that. It's a personal pet peeve of mine, all right?

—— 《Hawaii Five O 01x10》

✅ 客訴吃不好

記得有次一個同行跟我聊到峇里島時，說客人沒吃到蟹管裡面的肉當場沒說，後來才抱怨吃的不好。我心想峇里島不是吃螃蟹生蠔海灘BBQ吃到飽，怎麼會吃不好了？至於蟹管裡面的肉…餐盤旁邊不是有根木棍，拿起來敲啊～他說菲律賓才有木棍，印尼餐館沒給那棍子，我說那你拿刀叉或海邊撿塊石頭也可以敲啊，為了一根蟹管你們…考慮過螃蟹的感受嗎？！

你跟女學生在辦公室網聊的時候，有沒有考慮過我的感受？
How do you think I feel when I come into your office and you're instant messaging with a student?

—— 《Chloe》

我完全不考慮你的感受。
I'm completely disregarding your feelings.

—— 《Everybody Loves Raymond 02x12 All I Want For Christmas》

司領餐 "working lunch"

司領餐看什麼國家什麼地方,有些導遊不吃的。用餐時實習導遊、導遊助理和司機通常不會參與話題。所以是領隊跟導遊的一個小型會議,聊的多半是行程安排,客人反應,購物問題。無論遇到什麼問題,就記得人心是肉做的,能幹旅遊業的一般EQ也不會太低,只要你設身處地為對方著想,總能找出一個解決之道的。

給點指引?你只需要看著某人設身處地去想。

Any pointers? You just look at somebody and think like they think.

—— 《True Detective 01x03》

站在我的立場想想,科爾。

Put yourself in my place, Cole.

—— 《24Hrs 08x09》

4.5 印航假期 熱情海洋峇里島、按摩通通脫掉

情境對話

MP3 021

麥可
我們要一起去水療館按摩。
We are going to a spa and have massages together.

麥可
夢幻SPA館到了。
Here's the fancy Spa.

麥可
12歲以下的小朋友不能給你按摩喔。
They don't accept kids under twelve.

麥可
一小時的指壓。半開放式的房間。
Shiatsu one hour. A half-enclosed room.

麥可
房間的對面呢，是一片山壁，風景很美。
On the opposite room, it's a mountain wall. You've got a great view.

Henry
他們會在我身上塗很多按摩油嗎？
Will they apply a lot of massage oil onto me?

麥可
是的，全身。
Yep, the whole body.

Henry
那我的內褲可以脫掉嗎？
Can I remove my boxer shorts?

不客氣。
You are more than welcome.

我放棄。
I'll pass.

妳確定？
You sure?

我的肚子很怕癢。
My tummy is terribly ticklish.

好吧，但你知道不能退錢也不能轉讓。
Okay, but no refunds and it's nontransferable you know.

喔，我知道。這裡有腳底按摩嗎？
Oh, I know. Do they have foot massages?

這裡沒有。
They don't have them here.

那我自己玩手機好了。
Then I'll just play with my phone.

大家注意聽，如果你真的需要抓重龍。
Listen up, if you wanna have a real power massage.

你就說，「用力」。
You say, "harder."

小力一點你就說雅咩爹（誤）如果你要告訴她輕一點…
If you wanna tell her to lighten up a little…

就說「輕一點」。
Say "Easy."

麥可

沒有其他問題了吧？

Are we good?

Henry

她除了給我按摩還會…給一些其他那種的服務嗎？

She will give me a massage and… perform a few extra those extra services?

麥可

恬恬閉嘴好好按你的摩。

Just shut up and rub.

麥可

有人要指定男按摩師嗎？沒有嗎？那就跟著你的按摩小姐走。

Any one need a masseur [mæ'sɚ]? No? Then you just follow your personal masseuse [mæ'sɚs].

麥可

你覺得怎樣？

How do you feel?

Henry

剛才那個按摩真的是非常專業。

It was an extremely professional massage.

麥可

等一下可以多喝點水。

Drink lots of water after.

Henry

她的技術非常給力，還給我做了個頭皮按摩爽的要命。

She gave me the most amazing massages on the massage table, and she also gave me a scalp massage to die for.

Henry

這位按摩小姐應該可以得個什麼抓龍獎的。

This masseuse might just get a prize in rubbing.

麥可

你願意的話可以給點小費，她會很高興的。

You can tip her if you want to. She will be so happy.

麥可

好了，都到齊了。我們要走了。

Well, here we all are. We are leaving.

☆ 單詞與句型

✅ 怕癢 "ticklish"

Tickle spot、ticklish spot，就是容易會癢，敏感的那個點。比如有的人是腳底板，有的人是腋下，翻成笑點？不對，笑穴，不對，癢穴（咦）有點接近了但總覺得怪怪的好像哪裡不對…敏感點，暫時就這個了。會癢哦 "that tickles"，癢的要死 "It tickles like crazy." 還有抓癢那隻抓耙子怎麼說呢？"itch stick, back scratcher"，桿子還帶伸縮的？"extensible back scratcher"。

➜ itch

會癢好吧？

It itches, okay?

—— 《Bones 04x13》

我的眼睛有點癢。

My eye is a little itchy.

—— 《Friends 05x22 The One With Joeys Big Break》

➜ scratch

搔癢 "scratch"，會癢 "scratchy"。

他搔搔鼻子。

He scratches his nose.

—— 《Boardwalk Empire 1x07 Home》

我的嗓子有點癢。

My throat's a little scratchy.

—— 《*Everybody Loves Raymond 05x10 The Sneeze*》

你怕癢嗎？但我不覺得你會怕癢。走開！別碰我！

Are you ticklish? But I don't think you're tickly. Get off! Get off!

—— 《*Where The Streets Have No Name*》

有時大人玩小孩的時候，或情侶之間，會有 "**a tickle fight**"，這個中文怎麼翻？eh…抓癢…撓癢…呵癢大亂鬥好了。

就像是看小孩子的呵癢大亂鬥。

It's like watchin' the kids have a tickle fight.

—— 《*Everybody Loves Raymond 06x11 The Kicker*》

將會有一場呵癢大亂鬥。

There's gonna be a big tickle fight.

—— 《*Everybody Loves Raymond 06x11 The Kicker*》

→ 同場加映

你吃這個也癢，吃那個也癢。

Getting anything in your mouth makes you allergic and scratchy. / Anything you put in your mouth is gonna make you allergic and scratchy.

—— 《*Chu Ke-Liang*》

✔ 自己玩手機 "phubbing[fʌ•bɪŋ]"

phubbing表示自顧自滑手機無視他人，這個字是電話 "phone" 跟冷落、無視、愛理不理 "snub" 的組合字。你是低頭族嗎？"Are you a phubber?" 跟這個字常一起出現的句子有：別再低頭 "Stop phubbing"。你可以別再玩手機無視我了嗎？"Would you stop phubbing me?"

她已讀不回，目前我自己好空虛又被她人冷落。
She got my message and is choosing not to call me. Now I'm needy and snubbed.

—— 《Friends 01x20》

我看到她跟她學習小組的朋友在一起，對我完全無視。
I saw her with her study group friends, and they totally snubbed me.

—— 《Hot In Cleveland 04x03 Method Man》

✔ 短翹鼻的／短管左輪手槍 "snub-nosed"

她臉上有著可愛的翹鼻子和一雙楚楚動人的大眼睛 "She had an face with a snub nose and large appealing eyes."

我手裡的短管左輪，轟開你的下巴。
The snub in my paw, shove it in your jaws.

—— 《D12 Fight Music》

✔ 沒有其他問題了吧？ "Are we good?"

意思是沒問題了吧，跟中文一樣，沒問題也有兩種含意。

→ 一種是就事論事說得很清楚沒問題了。

但是我們今晚很缺人手，我本身還得去吧台幫忙，所以我才會安排你來工作。那麼…說的很清楚了吧？

But we're way understaffed tonight. I even have to man the bar. So that's why I scheduled you to work. So... Are we good?

—— 《He's Just Not That Into You》

→ 一種是指我們之間沒有誤會了，和好了，不處在敵對狀態了。

我們之間沒事吧？我們可以忘記過去這些不重要的事，然後互相信任，互相幫助嗎？沒事。

Are we good? And we can put all this other nonsense behind us and trust one another and continue to help one another? Yeah.

這樣很好，那狀況解除了。

I'd like that. Then consider the slate clean.

—— 《House Of Cards 02x01》

那…咱倆沒事吧？嗯，沒事。

So-o-o, are we good? Yeah. We good.

—— 《2 Broke Girls 1x03 And Trokes Of Goddwill》

✔ You are good to go.

附帶說明一下這句也很簡單常用又地道，"Are good to" 就是準備好可以去做什麼了。比如早上上學前孩子吃完早餐，媽咪幫他擦擦嘴角，然後說 "You are good to go." 你準備好可以出門了。用在大人身上，軍事電影裡也有看過，檢查配槍什麼的，然後班長對士兵說 "You are good to go."

我們能開始了嗎？對，馬上開始。

Are we good to go? Yes, move now.

—— 《24Hrs 08x07》

✔ 輕一點 "Easy. / Lighten up a little."

兄弟！別太用力。

Man! Not so hard.

—— 《Cougar Town 2x05》

很好，但是甩頭髮的時候放輕點。

Good, but easy on the hair flip.

—— 《2 Broke Girls 02x03》

✔ 按摩／抓龍 "massage / rubbing"

上面的按摩技術都說好的，那要形容不好的呢？

她那按摩技術爛到不行！

She gives the worst massages ever!

—— 《Friends 05x13 The One With Joeys Bag》

你的按摩技術世界無敵爛。

You give the worst massages in the world.

—— 《Friends 05x13 The One With Joeys Bag》

最佳的不會按摩獎…誰會得獎？

For the best bad-massage…Who would get that?

—— 《Friends 05x13 The One With Joeys Bag》

✅ 爽的要命 "to die for"

能擁有的話死了都值，棒的要命的。

上帝倒是給了她傲人的胸部和迷死人的雙腿。但那張臉不行！

God gave her one hell of a rack and legs to die for, though. But her face!

—— 《Shameless Us 02x02》

我有一個死了都要愛的老婆。

I have a wife to die for.

—— 《The Secret 2006》

✅ 都到齊了 "Here we all are."

人都算齊了嗎？

Is everyone accounted for?

—— 《American Horror Story 02x03》

 達人提點

✅ 年齡限制

部分旅行社是說12歲以下的小朋友不能按摩，另16歲以下也不建議，主要是考慮到青少年骨骼發育。有些旅行社則是不分12、16歲，凡16歲以

下的都不包含SPA療程，這種通常都會附上亦不可轉讓或要求退費的條款。或表明是贈送項目所以恕不退費 "No exchange or refund policy since it's a free item."

魔術是沒有年齡限制的。
You're never too old for magic.

—— 《Hawaii Five O 03x23》

什麼意思無法退費？我能找別的時間再去嗎？
What do you mean. It's nonrefundable? Can I just come some other time?

—— 《Friends 09x19 Rachel's Dream》

✅ 男按摩師 "masseur" ；按摩小姐 "masseuse"

眾口難調，有些人抓很重，不重不過癮，這個可以請問他要不要選男按摩師，下手會重一點，不過有些地方指名男按摩師要另外加錢。有的人就要輕的，都已經交代按摩小姐輕一點，客人還是覺得痛得要死再也不按了。有人去按摩遇過會推銷精油敷背什麼的，這種跟團一般不會發生。

這力度怎麼樣？
How's the pressure?

—— 《Hot In Cleveland 04x11 Fast And Furious》

小地方做巡警賺得不多，所以我做兼職按摩師餬餬口。
Being a ranger in a small town doesn't pay much, so I'm a part-time masseur to make ends meet.

—— 《Hot In Cleveland 04x11 Fast And Furious》

✅ 腳底按摩 "foot massage"

‹i.e.› foot rubs，腳底按摩也作foot reflexology（腳底穴道按摩），有些人很喜歡，但是要注意葡萄球菌感染 "staph infection"，如果身體抵抗力弱或腳上有傷口就不適宜。還有就是修腳皮，一般旅行社不會安排這種，但如果是自由活動的時間，晚餐後自己或跟著朋友一起去的，對於之前沒有作過或很少修腳皮的人最好避免，有些服務生修得太多刮得太深，曾經遇過客人弄完以後痛到沒法走後面的行程。

我20歲時得過葡萄球菌感染。

I got staph at 20.

—— 《2 Broke Girls 1x15 And The Blind Pot》

技擊手在他們訓練後用這個擦拭全身，能殺死蘚菌、葡萄球菌、抗藥性金黃色葡萄球菌。

Fighters use these to wipe down after they train. Uh, kills ringworm, staph, MRSA.

—— 《Hawaii Five O 02x06》

4.6

馬新3樂園
樂高水上樂園

情境對話

MP3 022

麥可

各位，記得帶上泳衣。
Hey Guys, bring your swimming suit with you.

Phelps

麥可，今天我們去玩水嗎？我擔心防曬霜沒塗夠…
Michael, will we go to a pool today? I guess I'm not wearing enough sunblock…

麥可

他們有室內泳池。
They have indoor pools.

麥可

如果你要玩室外滑水道，你可以用我的防曬霜。
If you wanna have fun at a water slide park outside, you can use mine.

Phelps

人很多吧，嗯？
Some turnout, uh?

麥可

還好吧，不會擠。
It's okay. Not much of a crowd.

麥可

好啦，到了。你可以就在那裡面換衣服。
All right. You're here. You can change your clothes in there.

那裡有付費衣櫃，按小時收費。
Lockers are available for rent in the locker room, you pay by the hour.

我的手錶也可以放裡面嗎？
Is it ok if I put my watch in here?

我猜可以吧，我看這衣櫃有強化設計。
I guess so. It think this locker has a sturdy enough design.

你的是什麼手錶？
What kind of watch do you have?

百達翡麗。
Patek Philippe ['pɛ•tɪk,fɪ•lɪp].

這個…那請你朋友幫你保管吧。
Well... Then you might wanna ask your friend to take care of it.

現在可以下水了嗎？
Can we get in the pool now?

等等，我在找生死狀。
Wait a moment, I'm looking for the disclaimer forms.

什麼？！
Say what?!

開玩笑的，你很安全的，沒事。
Just kidding. You are perfectly safe. You are okay.

真心話大冒險，你沒講真心話，但我要大冒險了。
Seriously, you aren't telling the truth, but I'm going out on a limb.

Phelps

嗚呼！一起來玩，麥可。
Whoo-hoo! Join me, Michael.

麥可

我在上班，你去玩的開心點。
My job. You go and have fun.

Phelps

有套手上的浮圈嗎？救生圈？
Any arm flouties? Swim rings?

Phelps

我剛才滑了一下差點跌倒。
I slipped and nearly fell.

Phelps

我不喜歡這Fu。
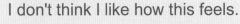
I don't think I like how this feels.

麥可

Hold住，頭抬起來然後呼吸。
Brace yourself, keep your head up and now breathe.

麥可

有救生員的啦，不用擔心。
There is a lifeguard boy. You gotta nothing to worry about.

Phelps

他帥麼？
Is he hot?

麥可

他相貌可不凡了。
He is so freaking hot.

麥可

奇怪自動販賣機在哪裡…
I wonder where the vendor is…

Phelps

你要去哪裡？壯士留步～～
Are you going somewhere? Don't you leave me~ ~

麥可

阿就放輕鬆就好了，你是在緊張什麼？
C'mon just give in to it, why are you freaking out?

好吧，我來幫你。
Okay, let me help you.

天靈靈地靈靈…斷開魂結！斷開鎖鍊！
Abracadabra… unshackled! Breaking off your mental chains!

天啊～哪有領隊這樣的…
Gosh~ What kinda tour manager do I have here…

說真的，你是誰派來的？
Honestly, who sent you?

不要問很恐怖。
You don't wanna know.

☆ 單詞與句型

✅ 保管 "take care of"

保管：keep、to take care of。就這麼簡單。不用太糾結字典上那種一對一的翻譯，試試一對多，多對一，你會發現講起話來就不像是在背書了。

所以我就替你保管了，省得你麻煩。

So I kept it so you wouldn't get in trouble.

　　——《*Everybody Hates Chris 1x05 Everybody Hates Fat Mike*》

判決前都由他們來保管。

They could take custody until verdict is reached.

　　——《*Franklin And Bash 02x03*》

我幫你保管個硬幣吧（在這裡是敲竹槓，恐嚇取財）。

Let me hold a quarter.

—— 《Everybody Hates Chris 02x01》

✅ 生死狀 "disclaimer forms"

聲明書，同意書，consents、permission slip。交班資料裡通常會附上幾種同意書 "Disclaimer forms"，比如：脫隊同意書，行程變更同意書，水上活動同意書，以備不時之需。團體名單事先多印2份（來回）給免稅店，免得還要麻煩店員丟下各種擠著結帳趕飛機的客人，跑去辦公室影印。分房表多印幾份，還沒能到旅館前台影印，一上車導遊就會要。

什麼？這是什麼？同意書。

What? What's this? Permission slip.

—— 《Shameless Us 01x10》

她們父母都已經簽署同意書了嗎？嗯，都簽了。

Have the girls' parents signed consents? Uh, yes to the consents.

—— 《Perception 02x04》

綜合瘦多小姐的證詞和簽過字的同意書以及離婚文件，我傾向認為索托小姐是那個最適合的人選。

Given Miss Soto's testimony and the signed consent forms and divorce papers, I'm inclined to rule that Miss Soto was that person.

—— 《Franklin And Bash 02x08》

我們讓我們的捐贈者在生前簽了一份同意書。

We get our donors to sign specific consent forms when they're alive.

—— 《Franklin And Bash 02x08》

✅ 我要大冒險了 "I'm going out on a limb."

膽顫心驚。一般想到冒險，就想到It's risky.或是It's dangerous.，但是口語上你可以説 "I'm going out on a limb[lɪm]." limb是樹枝，picture it（這樣想好了）你爬樹時爬到小樹幹上去了，在這種情境下，你會不會心驚膽顫小樹枝什麼時候會斷？這種一顆心懸在那裡的緊張感，就是go out on a limb了。

這件事情我打算賭一把。

I'm going to go out on a limb here.

—— 《American Horror Story 02x03》

✅ 嗚呼 "Whoo-hoo"

擬聲詞。Woot，woo，whooo都可以，擬聲詞看得懂就行沒什麼絕對正確的拼法可言，後面也可加個Hoo，例如 Woo Hoo。Whoo-hoo也可以。老外夜店裡派對上，總少不了Woo girl。打遊戲過關了，也可以來一句 "I defeated the dark sorcerer! Woot!" 我打敗了暗黑魔法師！

各位加油在舞池盡情跳吧，來吧，呼-呼！

Come on, everybody, hit the dance floor. Come on, whooo-whooo!

—— 《Skins 01x09 The Last Episode》

為什麼我聽到歡呼聲　沒事，是足球賽？

Why am I hearing cheering It's okay. It's just a football game?

—— 《Friends 09x07 Ross's Inappropriate Song》

讓我們為媽媽歡呼，舉起手來…耶～～

Let's hear it for Mommy. Raise your hand for... Yeah~ ~

—— 《Everybody Loves Raymond 01x02 I Love You》

她跟一群玩嗨的女生在一間叫做天旋地轉不要停的酒吧裡。

She's at that bar Giddyups with a bunch of Woo Girls.

—— 《How I Met Your Mother 04x08 Woooo》

✔ 我在上班 "My job."

職責所在。上班中，執勤中可以説on duty（不用加the，不用説on the duty，直接説on duty就可以了）。**比較** 出勤表，執勤人員名冊是the duty roster。

我執勤的時候不能喝酒，夫人。

I can't drink on duty, ma'am.

—— 《House Of Cards 02x10》

他在執勤的時候負傷了，我就知道這些。

He was on duty, he got hurt, that's all they would tell me.

—— 《Everybody Loves Raymond 04x15 Robert's Rodeo》

我還是個小男孩的時候，我每晚都趴在游泳圈裡看你們表演。

As a boy, I watched your set from the water wings every night.

—— 《Pushing Daisies 02x13》

✔ 救生圈 "swim ring"

游泳圈，水桶腰，啤酒肚 "A beer gut"，鮪魚肚，肚子上一圈肥肉，中文的形容詞很多，英文則可以説 "Love handles, muffin top"，如果指真的游泳圈救生圈是 "Swim ring"，英文裡的tuna belly沒有鮪魚肚的弦外之音 "An alternative meaning"。**例如** 這個夏天他的整個打擊肚子肥肉計畫以失敗告終了 "This summer his entire operation muffin top just went south."

我們一起喝出啤酒肚，我們也一起減肥吧。或者我們戒了啤酒。

We put on under beer weight together, we might take it off together. Or we could just stop drinking beer.

別！我說我們去健身房吧。

No! I say we join a gym.

—— 《*How I Met Your Mother 03x10 The Yips*》

✅ 救生員 "a pool boy"

Lifesaver是救命裝備，救命恩人，救世主，救命稻草，多虧了你這意思。那種六塊腹肌會做人工呼吸還順便抓抽菸的救生員，比較正式的說法是Life Guard，其他還有Baywatcher。有個美劇叫Baywatch，中譯《海灘遊俠》，是美國NBC電視台在1989年－2001年間播出的電視劇，男主角是1982年至1986年間《霹靂遊俠》*Knight Rider* 裡的那個德裔美國人，台譯李麥可的大衛・赫索霍夫 "David Michael Hasselhoff" 主演的，他還在海綿寶寶 "Sponge Bob Square Pants" 中演過自己。

沒有救生員，出事誰負責。

No lifeguard. Liability.

—— 《*Shameless Us 02x04*》

如果救生員看到，會把你趕出海灘。

The lifeguards are going to kick you off the beach if they see you.

—— 《*Hawaii Five O 02x04*》

噢，咖啡，我的救命稻草來的正是時候。

Oh, coffee. Lifesaver.

—— 《*Secret Diary Of A Call Girl 04x02*》

哦，謝謝你。你救了我的命。

Oh, thank you. You are a lifesaver.

—— 《*The Big Bang 02x16*》

但我的車在店裡，然後我在**45**分鐘內必須趕到環球影城。好吧，嗯，我載你。

But my car is in the shop, and I have to be at Universal in 45 minutes. Okay, well, I'll take you.

喔，你真是個救世主。

Oh, you're a lifesaver.

—— 《*The Big Bang 02x19*》

達人提點

進交班室前

唭唭切克鬧～公司OP要護照～吊牌繫繩護照套～拿了護照接下來交班室做手工，檢查護照效期 "EXPIRE DATE"，看OP資料好沒，如果還沒好，問清楚還缺什麼，比如PNR？還是團體合約書？搞清楚缺什麼後註明在交班單上，先拿其他資料，缺的等一下補，如果一直沒消息就請OP來交班室我跟你談談人生理想（大誤），如果還有什麼問題就請教團控（行李吊牌：Baggage Card；行李牌繫繩：Baggage Card String；護照的保護套：passport case）。

進交班室後

分房表 "rooming List"，大表 "Control List"，交叉比對看看誰是誰的誰。PNR對照交班單人數，LOCAL電話，自帶護照，外國護照，航班，機場，住哪裡吃什麼，交班單有沒有註明要出團前領取預繳服務費或簽證費的，注意一下公司出納的領款時間。

✅ 特別要求

3PAX，3 Passengers，connecting room（三位旅客。需求機位靠窗及相鄰房）。*Okie Dokie*

DOB，Date of Birth（壽星打星號）。*Got it*

前註INF，後註並沒有BBML（BABY兩歲以下不佔位不用餐免票）。*Uh-huh*

前註CHD，Child。後註並沒有CHML（小朋友吃正常餐）。*了解*

行前電話說明會，機上會冷帶外套，水上活動帶拖鞋，幾點集合幾號櫃，外幣要換多少錢。

✅ 紅十字會

如果大家對救人一命，義不容辭 "without any hesitation" 的話，可以去紅十字會報名受訓當救生員，結訓後會給證書，期限3年要再複訓 "recurrent training"。

4.7

終章
挑過骨頭的雞蛋一定是破的、且行且珍惜

情境對話
 MP3 023

麥可

在今天的聚餐看到各位真開心。介紹一下這位是阿芬，有很豐富的臨場經驗，有什麼問題要問她嗎？

Nice to meet you guys at the associates dinner. This is Jenny, she had a lot of field experience, any questions?

阿芬

大家好我是阿芬。等一下我們輪流自我介紹，一起認識認識。

Hi, everyone I am Jenny. Later let's introduce ourselves, and make some new friends here.

Angela

阿芬。我投履歷都沒人回。

Jenny. No responses to my resume.

阿芬

去跑業務。

Join the sales team.

Angela

聽説幹這行沒有退休金也沒有年終獎金。

I heard there's no pension or any year-end bonus in this line of business.

阿芬

是的。

Yup.

Angela

有些人還會從頭到尾吹毛求疵，只為了找個藉口不付服務費？
Some people are nitpicking the whole tour, just to find some lame excuse not to pay the cover charge? Is that true?

阿芬

咳咳。問得好。大部分人不會這樣的。
Cough Cough. Good question. Usually people don't act like that.

Angela

聽說只要有人客訴你就可以改行了。
I heard that once a customer files a complaint you are out of this business.

阿芬

只有沒帶過團的領隊才沒有客訴。
Only people who have never guided a tour before get complaints.

阿芬

預防勝於治療，多看看客訴案例，你會進入佳境的。
Prevention is better than cure. Read some more complaint cases, you're bound to get better.

Angela

淡季沒團帶，那我要幹什麼呢？
You have no job during slow times, then what?

阿芬

沒簽專任的是這樣。
If you're a freelancer, yes.

阿芬

機會是給有準備的人，各國語言學幾句。這行需要的不是專才，而是通才。
I'll say luck's being when opportunity knocks. Try to learn some different languages. No need to be a specialist in a business like ours, being a well-rounded person is more important.

Angela

我口才不好，我想放棄。
I'm not a good talker. I give up.

阿芬

拿出愚公移山的精神來，學的別都還給老師了。
Show me your spirit, remember your training.

Angela

麥可你今天怎麼這麼安靜，都不像你。
Michael why are you so quiet? This isn't you.

麥可

我特意空著肚子來吃大餐的…你有沒有看到這些生猛的螃蟹！？
I was purposely saving my stomach for the feast... You see these happy crabs!?

阿芬

他一直在看那個水族箱。
He has been gazing at the aquarium the whole time.

Angela

萬一我說的英文人家聽不大懂怎麼辦？
What if they don't understand half the words I am saying?

麥可

試著用不同方式來解釋，不要同樣的話一直跳針。
Try to express yourself in different ways, don't be verbally repetitive [rɪ'pɛ•tɪ•tɪv].

Angela

可以用一句話總結你的心得送給大家什麼好建議嗎？
A simple remark to give out some great tips?

麥可

不要凝視深淵太久，不然深淵也會開始凝望你。
Don't try to control everything, or everything will control you.

Angela

再說一遍？
Come again?

麥可

一切有為法，如夢幻泡影…
Ashes to ashes, destiny to destiny; swift as a shadow, short as any dream...

Angela

夠了，這位施主。你又開始鬼打牆了。說人話好不好？
Enough, sir. You're off-topic again. How about speaking English?

麥可

我也覺得。那就醬紫…了吧。以後我們就機場見了！
I think I am. That's it... Then. I'll see you at the airport!

Angela

壯士留步！說好的圖呢！
Halt! You promised me some pictures!

麥可

在臉書裡搜XBadaBing，有什麼好玩的也歡迎來粉絲團跟我一起分享。
Search XBadaBing on facebook, and facebook me cool things @ fan page :D

阿芬

好了好了。大家來輪流自我介紹吧，先從帥哥開始。
KK"Okay Okay." Let's go around and introduce ourselves. Start with the cute guys.

☆ 單詞與句型

✓ 履歷 "resume / résumé"

動詞發 [rɪ'zum]，名詞發 ['rɛzə,me]，把什麼什麼寫進，加進你的履歷裡用 "Add it to your resume." 加進的那點在你的履歷裡看起來不錯 "It would look good on that resume." 所以你的履歷就會讓人眼睛一亮了 "Your resume is quite impressive."

這日記就是我的簡歷。

That journal is my version of a resume.

—— 《*House Of Cards 02x05*》

我不是覺得她閱歷不夠，是她脾氣太怪了。

It's not her resume I have a problem with. It's her temperament ['tem•pɚ•rə•mənt].

——《Homeland 01x01》

追隨妥拉薩普學習三年現代舞？在美國芭蕾舞團待了五年？

Three years of modern dance with Twyla Tharp? Five years with the American Ballet Theatre?

誰的履歷表不灌水？

Everybody lies on their resume, okay?

——《Friends 03x12 All The Jealousy》

✓聽說 "I heard / I've heard / I heard about / I heard of"

Have you heard...聽過…？Haven't you heard...難道沒聽過…？！否定疑問句的語氣感覺更強，你沒聽説過不省思的人生活的不值得嗎？ "Haven't you ever heard that the unexamined life is not worth living?" 我聽説了！ "I heard!"這是蘇格拉底Socrates ['sɑ•krətiz] 的名言。

羅伯特，我都聽說了。

Robert, I heard about what happened.

——《Everybody Loves Raymond 04x15 Robert's Rodeo》

我聽說了你們很多事情。

I've heard so much about you.

——《Everybody Loves Raymond 05x08 Young Girl》

我從來沒聽說過這種事。

I've never heard of such a thing.

——《Everybody Loves Raymond 01x01 Pilot》

☑ 年終獎金 "year-end bonus" ；退休金 "pension / retirement fund / retirement money"

說到這裏，這是我的年終獎金支票。

As in, my end-of-the-year bonus check.

—— 《*How I Met Your Mother 06x12 False Positive*》

他們不得不找些兼職，有些人已經開始動用他們的退休金了。

They're having to take second jobs, people are dipping into their retirement funds.

—— 《*Everybody Loves Raymond 07x06 Robert Needs Money*》

☑ 吹毛求疵，nitpicking

"Split hairs" 頭髮那麼細，還要找分叉撕成兩縷？很有吹毛求疵那畫面吧。"persnickety" 主要是形容對細節太過計較，找盡麻煩難以應付這種感覺。"picking holes" 也是挑毛病的意思，hole或holes隨便不糾結單複數。

在此我不是要吹毛求疵，但這其實不是一本日記，而是筆記，是一本讀書筆記。

I don't want to split hairs here, but it's actually not a journal. It's a notebook. It's notes for a book.

—— 《*Girls 01x05*》

他太雞蛋裡挑骨頭了，簡直要把我逼的跳牆。

He's persnickety [pɝˈsnɪ•kə•tɪ]. It drives me up the wall.

—— 《*Modern Family 02x21*》

謝謝，理查，繼續糾結請自便。喂，新來的。該你了。

Thank you, richard, please resume picking your hole. Oi. Fresh meat. You're up.

—— 《Skins 05x01 Franky》

服務費 "the cover charge"

你給我們，恩，每人200塊。這個服務費是不是有點多啊。

You give us, uh, $200 per person. That's pretty steep for a cover charge.

—— 《How I Met Your Mother 07x14》

只要是我開的夜總會，哪怕要排隊三個小時他們都會來，而那些住在平民窟的人一分服務費也分不到。

People would stand in line for 3 hours if I opened a club, and no one who actually lives in the glades would see a penny of those cover charges.

—— 《Arrow 01x03》

口才 "good talker"

eloquence ['ɛ•lə•kwəns] 也是口才，不過口語中較少用到，他蠻會說話的 "He is good at talking / He knew how to talk." 他口才很好 "He is a smooth talker / He's a terrific speaker."

克里斯…你口才那麼好，你第一個上吧。

Chris... You're so very well-spoken. Why don't you go first?

—— 《Everybody Hates Chris 02x09》

她有應對生活中一切不順的智慧與口才，這才叫女人本色。

She has the wit and verbal acumen to handle anything life throws at her. That is a woman.

—— 《*Mixology S1x03 Bruce And Jessica*》

- Luck is when opportunity knocks and you answer ready. 機會是給有準備的人。
- 幫大家整理了幾句類似的名言 "famous sayings"：
  - "Chance favors only the prepared mind."

    ——Louis Pasteur.
  - "Luck is when opportunity runs into your effort by chance."

    ——Forrest Gump.
  - "Luck is when opportunity meets desperation."

    ——Steve Tobak.

✅ 不像你 "This isn't you."

要表達這種感覺的時候，有幾種用法，如果直接省略不用 "like" 這個字。

怎麼了？你在電話裡喊得像個瘋婆子。那可不像你。

What's the matter? You were yelling like a crazy lady on the phone. That's not you.

—— 《*Everybody Loves Raymond 08x18 Crazy Chin*》

→ 如果用 "**like**" 或 "**unlike**"

很抱歉我並不像你。

I'm sorry I'm not more like you.

—《*Girls 02x03*》

她有感恩的心，不像你，從不感謝我。

She likes to thank people Unlike you, who never thanks me.

—《*Cougar Town 1x07*》

→ 如果用 "**sound like**" 或 "**look like**"

這不像你啊。

That doesn't sound like you.

—《*Friends 10x08 The Late Thanksgiving*》

這不像你的作風。

This doesn't look like you.

—《*Payback 1999*》

✔聽不大懂 "don't understand half the words I am saying"

英語發音好不好，跟Siri聊聊就知道。如果覺得自己有口音方面的問題，上網搜Englishcentral，以前免費現在要錢，一個月十幾塊美金吧。每天玩幾個小時大概半年會感覺到明顯進步，這是我知道的最有效方式，比泡老外有效。

✅同樣的話一直跳針 "verbally repetitive" [rɪ'pɛ•tɪ•tɪv]

這表示她只是在語無倫次的重複說一些事情。

It could mean she reiterated [rɪ'ɪ•tɜ•ret] something out of order.

—— 《Stargate 04x05 Divide And Conquer》

你感到洩氣是因為他回覆時的表達方式只是一些無意義的重複措辭。

You're frustrated because he phrased his reply in the form of a meaningless tautology.

—— 《The Big Bang 02x03》

✅自我介紹 "introduce ourselves"

我來做個自我介紹開開場白吧 "Let me start by introducing myself. / Begin with introductions"。

抱歉，忘了自我介紹，艾希莉·愛默生，《她》雜誌的時尚編輯。

Sorry, didn't introduce myself. Ashley Emerson, style editor for Elle.

—— 《2 Broke Girls 1x19 And The Pring Break》

真抱歉我們還沒正式地自我介紹，我叫卡倫·博漢南，我在鐵路局工作。

I regret we haven't been properly introduced. Cullen Bohannon. I work for the railroad.

—— 《Hell On Wheels 01x03》

我們將從隊伍自我介紹開始，另一隊先，然後換你們。

Look, we're about to start with the team intros. The other team is up first and then you.

—— 《2 Broke Girls 02x04》

 達人提點

✓ 語言與禮儀

那麼多的語言當然學不完，但是也不要到了任何國家，一開口就劈哩趴啦落一堆英文。如果有空可以多學點幾種不同語言的比如你好對不起謝謝，這種簡單的，然後加上比如我德語／義語／法語／或什麼語說的不好，請問可以說英文嗎？這樣才有禮貌喔，也比較不會有人家明明聽的懂，但就是不想理你的情況發生，對你的態度也會好很多。若某種語言只想學一點簡單的，可以搜下Pimsleur，他除了英語，什麼語都教。雖然是用英語教第三外語，但是用字簡單，而且大部分都是重覆那些固定的話，聽起來沒什麼壓力不用擔心。偶而出現幾個生字就當作摸蛤仔兼洗褲，google下順便一起學了。

安安，我的義大利語不輪轉。不好意思，你講英語嗎？

Hello, I don't speak much Italian. Excuse me, do you speak any English?

"Buongiorno. (Io) non parlo molto l'italiano. Scusa, (Lei) parla inglese?"

一點點，怎麼幫您？

A little bit. How can I help you?

—— 《Pimsleur Italian》

✅ 小貼士

剛帶團的時候可以備個小紙條，有時忙別的事或睡覺時迷迷糊糊被叫起來，這紙條就有用了。一般問什麼時候交班幾位客人；若不是固定走某條線的可以問明航班 "Flight" 後上網先瞅瞅行程，爬文要注意發文時間，太舊的Post所描述的可能跟目前情況不同；freelance的話記下主管或OP大名，專線以備聯絡。

適不適合做這行？這個嘛…如果你想走，地球就是你的；如果你不想走，地溝油就是你的。跟生命中的很多其他事情一樣，同樣的事情隨著不同的人感受也不同，看你怎麼想。常有人説環遊世界還可以賺錢這樣太犯規，其實，如果單純愛旅遊，當客人就好了。最後補充 "As a side note"：風景是一回事，重點在陪你看風景的那個人。領隊是一個人看夕陽的。*smiles and go poof*

CHECKING LIST 附錄

斜背包 Messenger Bag

☐ 寫字板 clipboard	☐ 多層文件夾 pocket folders
☐ 手錶 watch	☐ 手機 cell phone
☐ 錢包 wallet	☐ 旅行支票 travelers checks
☐ 鈔票夾 money clip	☐ 小包面紙 pocket tissues
☐ 台幣 NT Dollar	☐ 美金 US Dollar
☐ 當地貨幣 local currency	☐ 牙線 floss
☐ 口氣清香劑 mint	
☐ 座墊紙 toilet seat cover / toilet sheet	
☐ 小藥盒 pill box （個人必備隨身藥品，請自由心證）	
☐ 行李箱鑰匙、密碼 luggage key, numbers to open your combination lock	
☐ 各種優惠卡 discount cards、貴賓卡 Priority Pass （機場貴賓室 airport lounges — 可吃免費冰淇淋^^）	
☐ 信用卡（預借現金密碼 cash advance pin、特約服務 engaged services）	
☐ A5筆記本（筆、釘書機 stapler、簡報稿 briefing note、買啥紀念品 souvenir、滑雪衣／發熱衣 baselayer、記各袋待補充事項）	
☐ 乾式洗手液 "hand sanitizers/alcohol rubs"	
☐ 護照、身份證（隨身帶反正不重也不佔地方，放托運行李會很麻煩）	

腰包 Fanny Pack

（比較不重要的、有重量的東西可以放腰包，然後斜背在背上。既能分散重量，又能避免有人覺得綁在腰上不時尚的問題。）

☐ 水壺 kettle	☐ 溼巾 wet-nap
☐ 吸油面紙 oil absorbing sheets	
☐ 衛生紙 tissue / toilet papers（廁所沒紙，路上流鼻水）	
☐ 行動電源 power bank（wifi很費電）、USB（線要長，才能電池放包，手拿著手機玩）	

登機箱、車包 Cabin Suitcase

☐ 領隊旗桿（領隊証）	☐ 錄音筆dictaphone
☐ 帽子、薄外套	☐ 咳嗽藥
☐ 隨車包背帶	☐ 旅行支票 travelers checks
☐ 自家鑰匙	☐ 備用眼鏡
☐ 提貨單（市區預購、機場提貨）**切記隨身帶不可托運。	
☐ 抽取式垃圾袋（**25cmx30cm 100 pieces**，用來車上吃吃喝喝）	
☐ 口香糖（司機打瞌睡或精神不濟時可派上用場）	
☐ 信封袋（行李小費、導遊對帳、出入境卡E / D、海關單C / D）	
☐ **ALT**手機（須事前查明當地**SIM**卡規格）	

隨船小包 Boat Bag

☐ 瓶裝水	☐ 防水袋	☐ 吐司（餵魚）
☐ 照相機（注意防水，海浪會出其不意直接打臉^^）		
☐ 塑膠袋裝點硬幣（給跳海小朋友）		

大行李 Check in baggage

行李底層

☐ 護照用照片（白色背景）3張
☐ 護照／簽証／台胞証／身份證影本（遺失補辦或臨時申請簽証用）， 旅行支票號碼存根

其他

☐ 免洗圓筷	☐ 拖鞋
☐ 抽取式垃圾袋（**30cmx45cm 300 pieces**，可放髒衣服、鞋子）	
☐ 廚房紙巾（出浴室可以擦腳、寄鋪缺毛巾也可以頂著先）	
☐ 泡麵（別帶多，只能帶出不能帶回）	

內褲襪子包

☐ 免洗內褲	☐ **Boxer**內褲	☐ 隱形襪
☐ 免洗襪	☐ 保暖襪	☐休閒短褲

自用藥包（外用）

☐ 口罩	☐ 防水OK絆	☐ 保險套
☐ 殺菌消毒水	☐ 口內膏（乾冷、壓力大、口角炎）	
☐ 酸痛貼布 　溼熱氣候用 "油性"（水性貼不住容易掉） 　乾冷氣候用 "水性"（油性的話會撕下一層皮）		
☐ 耳溫槍（**37.5℃－38.4℃**是低燒，物理降溫多喝水，以溫水（**37℃**） 　毛巾擦身體，**38.5℃**以上，服用退燒藥。）		

自用藥包（內用）

☐ 止咳藥	☐ 止痛藥	☐ 感冒退燒藥
☐ 腸（肚臍以下，用正露丸，純屬個人經驗）		
☐ 胃（肚臍以上，用胃散小袋式和胃乳小袋式，純屬個人經驗）		
☐ 維他命**B**提神		
☐ 大蒜精（防水土不服）		

工具箱1／2（電器）

相機推薦買有GPS的，回家後自動串起你的路線圖，還可以在GOOGLE MAP上逛一次

☐ 充電器（相機、手機、**PAD**）	☐ 行動分享器（**wifi**）
☐ 轉換插頭（**110vA**型／**220vC**型，**220v**注意粗細，最好是當地買的，細的不可接瓦數高的東西，別問我怎麼知道的，我不想說。）	
☐ 第二手機	
☐ **220v**延長線－要輕、線要短，兩人同房插頭不夠充，或集中管理避免忘記帶走。	

工具箱2／2（電器）

☐ 膠帶	☐ 美工刀	
☐ 各記憶卡	☐ **A4**檔案保護袋	☐ 防撞包
☐ 單據包從車包里的發票單據整理到這里，放沿路各種收集來的名片**DM**		
☐ 其他各充電器（注意不同接頭）		

盥洗包（**Toiletry Kits / Toiletry Bags**）

☐ 洗髮精	☐ 洗面乳	☐ 沐浴乳
☐ 棉花棒	☐ 溼巾	☐ 梳子
☐ 加寬**X3**小鏡子	☐ 漱口水	☐ 香水
☐ 防曬	☐ 沙拉 慕斯瓶	☐ 眼藥水（去紅眼）
☐ 保溼（**Hydrating**）減少流汗		

下機補充包（塞入托運行李的雙網間）

☐ 隱形眼鏡	☐ 隱形眼鏡用溼潤液	☐ 護唇膏
☐ 噴霧式乾式洗手劑（可洗手或去手指上煙味）		
☐ 折疊傘（有些國家不能帶上飛機，所以要放托運行李）		

☞ 下機後隨即在機場取出，放入隨車包，建議用較軟的**100ml**透明塑膠封口袋裝，才不會割破衣服或行李箱網子。

出發前（一般注意事項）

☐ 洗衣服	☐ 收衣服	☐ 關瓦斯
☐ 關電腦	☐ 剪指甲	☐ 剪髮
☐ 洗碗（洗碗槽裡的濾網丟掉）	☐ 上廁所	
☐ 檢查冰箱（在回來以後會過期的先吃掉）		
☐ 各充電器拔出帶上（最常忘記就是這個）		
☐ 倒垃圾（不然會回到一個臭臭的家喔）		
☐ 廣告信（請鄰居幫忙拿掉門口廣告信，以免信箱插了一堆廣告信，小偷會想 這家沒人在）		
☐ 檢查門窗（檢查門戶是否安全上鎖）		

出發前（若出國時間長）

製冷

☐ 噴在衣服上的涼感噴霧劑	☐ 瞬間涼感濕紙巾

蚊蟲

☐ （預防）防蚊液	☐ （止癢）蚊蟲咬傷止癢藥

寒帶包

☐ 防風衣	☐ 黏貼型暖暖包（生理期的好幫手）
☐ 緊身滑雪 衣、發熱衣	
☐ 薄的衛生棉（零下30度，用來貼鞋墊防結晶割腳）	
☐ 防滑鞋（下雪結冰的話地上真的很滑、普通的鞋很容易摔）	

長居、長飛（歐美線）

☐ 外語書籍 / 翻譯機	☐ 指甲刀（修容組）
☐ 眼罩	☐ 頸枕（neck／travel pillow）
☐ 安眠藥	☐ 國際駕照
☐ 國際學生證	
☐ 電腦、SSD碟、慣用滑鼠、耳麥、額外電腦設備	

Leader 011

導遊、領隊FUN英語

作　　者／Theodore
發 行 人／周瑞德
企劃編輯／劉俞青
執行編輯／陳韋佑
封面設計／高鍾琪
內文排版／菩薩蠻數位文化有限公司
校　　對／陳欣慧、饒美君

印　　製／大亞彩色印刷製版股份有限公司
初　　版／2015 年 1 月
出　　版／力得文化
電　　話／（02）2351-2007
傳　　真／（02）2351-0887
地　　址／100台北市中正區福州街 1 號 10 樓之 2
E m a i l ／best.books.service@gmail.com
定　　價／新台幣 360 元

港澳地區總經銷／泛華發行代理有限公司
地　　址／香港筲箕灣東旺道3號星島新聞集團大廈3樓
電　　話／（852）2798-2323
傳　　真／（852）2796-5471

國家圖書館出版品預行編目(CIP)資料

導遊、領隊"趣"英文 /
Theodore著
　— 初版. — 臺北市：
力得文化, 2015. 01
　　面；　公分. — (Leader ; 11)
　ISBN 978-986-91458-0-0(平裝附光碟片)

　1. 英語 2. 旅遊 3. 會話
805.188　　　　　　　　103026996

力得文化
Leader Culture

Lead your way. Be your own leader!

力得文化
Leader Culture

Lead your way. Be your own leader!